RYLAN

SEATTLE SASQUATCH HOCKEY
BOOK ONE

I0636980

M/M HOCKEY ROMANCE

HARPER ROBSON

2024

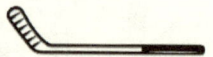

Content Information

Rylan's story touches on topics that may be difficult for some people. Please use your best judgement if any of these topics cause you stress. They include: an alcoholic parent, death of a parent (years earlier, not on page), death of a sibling (years earlier, not on page), and mention of homophobic behavior and language.

Thanks for reading, and I hope you enjoy Rylan's story.

Disclaimers

Being a lifelong hockey fan, I was surprised by how much I ***didn't*** know about how the world of professional hockey works. I've done my best to keep things realistic, but I did take some creative liberties! If I got any of the hockey rules or terminology wrong, please feel free to let me know by emailing harper@harperrobson.com

The use of the NHL and any of its teams are used as part of this work of fiction. This book does not reflect the policies or opinions of the actual organization known as the National Hockey League or any of its teams.

Names, characters, businesses, places, events, and incidents are either the product of the author's imag-

ination or are used in a fictitious manner. Any re-
semblance to actual persons, living or dead, or actual
events is purely coincidental.

Contents

All books are available on Amazon and in Kindle Unlimited

CHAPTER 1

RYLAN

The glass and steel facade of the Seattle Sasquatch's practice arena reflects the September sunshine, casting long shadows across the parking lot as I pull into my spot. My watch reads 7:45 AM, exactly fifteen minutes early, as usual. I'm nothing if not predictable. Training camp doesn't begin until tomorrow, but everyone on the team got a late-night notice to show up today for a mandatory pre-camp meeting. It's weird, but who am I to question? I'm just lucky I was in town. A lot of guys are taking advantage of our last few days of freedom by getting away with their families or girlfriends, but the message from our GM was clear: we're all expected to show up, either in person or by video call.

The familiar weight of responsibility settles across my shoulders as I grab the coffee from my truck's cup holder and head inside.

Photos and memorabilia from our team's short but eventful history line the walls outside the meeting room. Everyone's favorite picture is the on-ice shot taken in the moments after we won the Cup three years ago. It's a great photo, but right now, it's a constant reminder of expectations we haven't met since that first magical season.

Unsurprisingly, I'm the first one to arrive, so I grab my normal seat on the far side of the first row. Everything about this room screams high-end pro sports franchise, from the extra-wide leather chairs, arranged auditorium style, to how the team logo is subtly incorporated throughout the space. The room's front wall is dominated by a large multimedia screen, with smaller screens and electronic whiteboards scattered around the room.

My chair creaks as I settle in, steam rising from my coffee as I check my phone. No missed calls from my dad, thank god. Our last confrontation over his drinking still weighs heavy, but I push those thoughts aside. Right now, I need to focus on my job and try not to let my nerves show. You'd think that after more than a decade in the NHL, I'd have outgrown my beginning-of-season jitters, but you'd be wrong. Our team has a lot to prove after the disappointing last two seasons, and as captain, that burden falls squarely on my shoulders.

A couple of minutes later, Louis Tremblay, our number one goalie and my childhood best friend, walks in, a smile on his face, as usual. He drops into the seat beside me. "Dude, what's the deal with this meeting at the ass-crack of dawn before camp even starts? I'm on about three hours of sleep right now." He waggles his eyebrows.

I roll my eyes. "That's a shame for you. So, I take it that means last night's date went well?"

He gives me a filthy grin. "Oh, fuck yeah. This girl was gorgeous. I felt kind of bad leaving after we were done."

"Really?" I say. "I figured you'd be thrilled to get Carson's message. Gives you the perfect excuse to avoid hanging around."

He shrugs. "Eh, whatever. Maybe I wasn't that sad to leave. I'm just bitter about losing my last chance to sleep in for a while." He takes a sip from his own coffee. "But seriously, what the hell is this meeting about? That text was weird, right?"

It's my turn to shrug. "No idea. They didn't tell me anything."

My line-mate and friend Austin Coté strides into the room a moment later, followed by a clutch of other players, along with Kelly Garneau, the executive assistant to our General Manager, Carson Wells.

Some guys flash me nervous grins as they pass, while others bob their heads in greeting. Austin takes a seat behind us. "Hey," he says, his dark, assessing gaze taking everything in. When Kelly fires up the big screen, several of our other teammates have already connected to the video call, their faces looking like the opening sequence from *The Brady Bunch*, and there's some good-natured banter and ribbing while we wait.

When the commotion in the room has settled into an expectant hum, Carson Wells, our General Manager, and our new Head Coach, Travis Shaw, walk through the door.

Even though he's younger than most GMs in the league, Wells has a quality that commands respect. It might be the way he carries himself, or maybe it's that he's proven himself willing to make tough calls for the good of the team.

"Good morning, everyone," he says. "I know this is an unusual time for a team meeting, especially since training camp hasn't officially begun. Thank you all for making time to be here, whether in person or virtually."

He gestures to Travis Shaw, standing beside him. "Most of you have already met Coach Shaw, but for those who haven't had the chance yet, Travis comes to us from Florida's AHL affiliate. He's got eighteen seasons of NHL experience as a player, and we're excited to have him lead us this year."

Coach Shaw gives a brief nod of acknowledgment but doesn't speak. That's one thing I've noticed in the few interactions we've had so far: the man doesn't waste words.

"I know you're all wondering why we called this meeting," Carson continues. "We have some big news."

My stomach clenches. I scan the room, realizing there are a couple of guys missing. Louis shifts in his seat beside me, and tension radiates off Austin behind us.

"We made some significant changes to our roster late last night," he says, his tone measured. "We've completed a trade with the Florida Jaguars."

My heart pounds against my ribs. Trade announcements are always nerve-wracking. It means someone's not in this meeting because they're no longer part of our team.

"We've sent Liam Coulson and Darren Freeman, along with two prospects and our first-round pick for next year's draft, to Florida." Carson pauses, letting that sink in. A few muttered curses break the silence. Gino Santucci, one of our best defensemen, looks devastated—he and Liam have been best friends for ages.

"In   return," Carson continues, "we've   acquired Jamie Pirelli."

The room erupts in whispers, but for a moment, I can't hear anything over the sudden rush of blood in my ears. Jamie Pirelli. The first, and so far only, openly bisexual player ever drafted. I force my expression to remain neutral as my stomach twists.

My attention snaps back to our GM as he gives us the Cliff notes on our new teammate: he was a first-round draft pick three years ago. He was hailed as the next "Once In A Generation Player", the same way my older brother, Nick, was years ago. In Pirelli's case, the expected greatness hasn't materialized.

What our GM doesn't mention is Pirelli's reputation as a selfish player who's more concerned with his own stats than what's best for the team. Someone who causes endless drama, fights with his teammates, clashes with coaches and management, and treats everyone around him like shit.

A specific memory surfaces from a home game against the Jaguars last season when Pirelli threw himself in front of Gino Santucci's slapshot to protect his goalie. Gino's a defenseman with a wicked shot, so blocking it with his thigh must have hurt like hell, but Pirelli powered through, finishing his shift before limping off the ice. It didn't seem like the move of someone who only cared about his own personal glory.

But regardless of my observations of Jamie Pirelli, having him on our team is going to be complicated.

"In addition," Carson adds over the murmurs, "we're getting their farm-team goalie, Tanner Sinclair."

Louis's body stiffens beside me at that news.

"Pirelli and Sinclair will both be here tomorrow for the first day of camp," Carson says. "I expect everyone to make them feel welcome."

I glance around the room, taking in the mixed reactions. Some guys look excited, while others seem concerned. Austin's face behind me is unreadable, but his jaw is clenched. As captain, part of my job is to help smooth this transition, to make sure the team chemistry doesn't suffer too much from losing Liam and Darren, and to integrate these new players as quickly as possible.

Carson's gaze sweeps the room one final time. "Thanks for coming in early, everyone. The weight room's open if anyone wants to get a workout in." His mouth quirks up in a slight smile. "Obviously, that's not required since camp hasn't started yet. Union rules." He winks.

A few chuckles ripple through the room. Some guys are already standing, probably eager to hit the gym and work off some of the tension from this announcement.

"Rylan," Carson says, catching my eye. "Got a minute to meet?"

I nod, gathering my nearly empty coffee cup. Louis shoots me a questioning look as he stands, but I shrug. *Your guess is as good as mine, dude.*

The knot in my stomach tightens as I follow Carson to his office. I'm sure he just wants to talk about helping the new guys fit in, but my mind races as I try to sort out what this change means for the team.

I've spent thirteen years in the NHL building walls so high that I'm not sure I know who I am behind them anymore. The thought of this kid rolling in here and owning who he is without apologizing or hiding makes my chest ache with the familiar feeling of shame.

"Coffee?" Carson asks, moving to the fancy machine in the corner of his bright corner office while I take a seat in one of the leather club chairs by the window.

"No, thanks," I say. I don't think my nervous stomach would appreciate more caffeine at this point.

He takes a seat in the chair across from mine. Leaning forward to rest his elbows on his knees, he meets my eyes. "So? What are your thoughts?"

I hesitate. Carson's a great GM, and he's always encouraged us to be honest, even if he doesn't like what we have to say, but this situation is different. The decision's been made, the trade is done, and it doesn't matter what I think.

"Well... I'm not sure what to think yet, but I know you make all trade calls with the team's best interests in mind."

He shoots me a wry smile. "Very diplomatic, Captain. The PR folks would be thrilled, but right now, I want to talk honestly. This conversation will remain between us. I'd appreciate your honest opinion here."

I glance out the window over Carson's shoulder. The snow-capped Olympic mountains blur as I think about the disaster that was our last season. We spent most of the year at the bottom of the standings, without a snowball's chance in hell of making the playoffs. It was easily the worst season of my entire career, and I'm not eager to repeat it. I suck in a breath. "Well, the guys are frustrated and disappointed after the last couple of years." I clear my throat. "I'm a little concerned that bringing in someone like Pirelli could make the room a bit more... volatile." I swallow hard. "But we'll make it work," I add hastily.

Carson nods. "I understand your concerns. I'm well aware of Pirelli's reputation as a problem child. But Travis Shaw got to know him while he was down in Florida, and he's got a lot of confidence in the kid."

Carson leans back in his chair, rubbing a hand over his face. "Look, Rylan, I need to be straight with you about something. Ownership isn't happy."

Shit. Ownership being pissed is never a good thing.

"They wanted to blow the whole thing up after last season. They pushed to trade everyone except Tremblay and start fresh." He holds my gaze. "I fought hard to keep this group together. I was able to convince them that our core is solid, and a few strategic changes could make a huge difference."

My earlier coffee turns sour in my gut. Last season was awful, but I didn't believe we were that close to the team being dismantled. Since we're an expansion team, I hoped the world might cut us a little slack. Apparently, that's not happening. I guess winning the entire thing in our first season set some high expectations.

"This trade for Pirelli?" Carson continues. "It's a compromise. The owners wanted wholesale changes, I wanted minimal disruption. We met in the middle." He drums his fingers on the armrest. "But I'll be honest with you, Rylan. If things don't turn around fast, I might not be able to hold them back."

The weight of responsibility settles more heavily on my shoulders.

"How long do we have?" My voice comes out rough.

"Hard to say. But we need to show significant improvement by the All-Star break." His expression is grim. "They're not going to sit through another season like last year."

Well, that's pretty damn clear. The All-Star break is in February, about halfway through our 82-game season. Either we make this work—fast—or the team gets torn apart. *No pressure or anything.* I rub at my temple, feeling the beginning of a headache.

"According to Travis Shaw, Pirelli was in a difficult situation. The Jaguars..." Carson pauses, choosing his words carefully. "Well, I'm sure you've heard the rumors. Travis doesn't think the kid got a fair chance to show what he's capable of."

I've heard the rumors about the shit that goes on in the Jags' locker room. Everyone has. There's never been anything concrete, but it's enough to paint an ugly picture of a team that's very "old school". It wouldn't be the most welcoming team for an out, queer player. But Florida won the draft lottery that year, and Pirelli was unquestionably the best player. They would have had to out themselves as complete bigots if they'd passed him over. Taking anyone else would have made their prejudice obvious, and caused a PR shitstorm.

"Kid's got incredible natural talent," Carson says. "The Jaguars tried to force him to play their way, to be someone he's not. Here, we want our players to be themselves."

I swallow hard, the familiar guilt churning in my gut.

He clears his throat. "Because of the altercation he had with Belov, they were motivated to move him, so we got him for a lot less than he's worth."

I nod slowly. At the end of last season, there was a fight between Pirelli and their team's biggest star, a Russian powerhouse named Vladimir Belov, that was all over the hockey news.

"Travis believes Pirelli could be a real asset. But I won't lie, it's a risk," Carson continues. He runs a hand through his hair. "If Travis is wrong about him, or if Pirelli can't or won't leave his antics behind..." He lets the sentence hang.

He doesn't have to say the words. If this gamble doesn't pay off, it won't only be Pirelli's career on the line. It could be the final nail in the coffin for our whole team.

"I'll do everything I can to make it a smooth adjustment," I tell Carson, ignoring the knot in my gut.

Some of the tension leaves Carson's shoulders. "I know you will, Rylan. I'm counting on you to help get Pirelli on board. The guys respect your leadership. You've never let personal issues get in the way of what's best for the team."

If he only knew. My entire career has been built on keeping my *'personal issues'* locked away, deep in the darkness of the closet.

"Whatever you need from me." My words are automatic. Being the captain means putting the team first, no matter what. Even when it means welcoming someone whose presence makes me question things about myself I've spent years trying to ignore.

But this isn't about me or my... *issues*. I square my shoulders. "We'll make it work."

I just wish I felt as confident as I sound.

CHAPTER 2

JAMIE

The rental car's leather steering wheel is cool under my palms as I look through the windshield at the sleek architecture of the Seattle Sasquatch's practice rink and training complex. My new team clearly spared no expense with this place; it's a showpiece, unlike the practice rink in Florida, which was banished to some random warehouse district that even GPS had trouble finding.

My phone buzzes with a text from my sister Lola, back in Boston.

Dude, you got this.

A smile tugs at my lips, despite the butterflies in my stomach. Lola's always in my corner. My whole family is the same way. They back me up no matter what, even if they don't understand why I do half the things I do. We're tight-knit, but man, it's hard not to feel like the black sheep sometimes. They're all very academic and cerebral, with their noses buried in research and dissertations, laser-focused on climbing career ladders, or, in my parents' case, being well-respected in their academic worlds.

Meanwhile, I've always been the extroverted jock who'd pick tossing a ball around with my buddies over hitting the books. The social butterfly who thrives on team spirit and sunshine. Talk about not fitting the family mold. Maybe that's why getting frozen out by my Florida teammates cut me so deep. Sometimes, it's hard to feel like I belong anywhere.

Nope, not gonna go down that rabbit hole. Today is all about fresh starts and new beginnings. A clean slate, or whatever other cliché you want to plug in there.

My leg bounces as I stare at the building, working up the courage to go inside. I wasn't supposed to arrive in Seattle until late tonight, but after I got the official word of my trade, I grabbed an earlier flight. I was eager to get the fuck out of Florida.

After my teammate Vladimir Belov beat the crap out of each other at the end of last season, I knew I was done with the Jaguars, so I got my shit together and dealt with a lot of moving details early. I spent my entire summer waiting for a trade. Unfortunately, I didn't get to find out where I was going to play this year until yesterday. There's nothing quite like getting one day's notice to move from one corner of the USA to the other, but hey, I'm not about to complain about leaving that shitty experience in my rearview mirror. This is a fresh start, and there is no *fucking* way I'm going to screw up this chance.

I know I'm a damn good hockey player, but unless I tone down my antics and my admittedly bad attitude, I probably won't get another chance in this league. I've burned some bridges during the last three years, so the pressure is on for me to prove myself. It's now or never.

Deep breath... I can do this.

The crisp autumn air fills my lungs as I walk across the parking lot—a delightful contrast to Florida's sticky humidity.

The glass doors whoosh open, and I hitch my backpack over my shoulder as I step through. Four pristine ice rinks stretch out before me. There's a bright atrium straight ahead of me where a bunch of kids are playing on a jungle gym while their adults chat and drink coffee on sleek benches. A skate shop sits behind the play area.

Okay, this is it. Time to show them who Jamie Pirelli really is, not who the Jaguars made me out to be.

I head up the wide glass staircase to the second-floor offices. A young woman with a blonde pixie cut sits at the reception desk, and she greets me with a bright smile.

"Hi there. How can I help you?"

"Hey, I'm Jamie Pirelli." I smile politely at her. "I'm—"

Her blue eyes widen as she recognizes my name. "Oh my gosh, I know who you are! Hi Jamie, I'm Riley Campbell. It's so great to meet you." She jumps up from her chair and comes around the reception desk, extending her hand, her smile growing warmer. "I work in PR, but I'm helping out in reception this afternoon. I didn't realize you were coming in today."

I shake her hand, relief coursing through me—at this point, I'll take any friends I can find. "Well, I wasn't supposed to be here till tomorrow, but I got an earlier flight. I was hoping either Carson Wells or Travis Shaw would have some time for me."

"Of course, just let me check." She hustles back around the desk and grabs the phone. After a quick conversation, she looks up at me. "Coach Shaw will be right down. I'm so sorry; we weren't expecting you until tomorrow with the rest of the guys. Otherwise, I would have had everything ready for you."

"No, don't apologize; I'm here way early." I give her my most charming smile, grateful for her genuine warmth. *So far, so good.*

A couple of minutes later, Travis Shaw strides into the reception area, a broad smile on his handsome face.

Coach Shaw was one of the few bright spots during my time with the Jags. He coached our team's AHL affiliate, otherwise known as the farm team. But Florida's farm team plays in the same city as their 'parent' team, so there's a lot of interaction. Travis and I clicked right away. He always treated me like a person, not a problem to be managed. Without Travis, I probably wouldn't have lasted as long as I did on the Jags.

"Jamie Pirelli!" his smile reaches his eyes as he pulls me in for a quick bro-hug. "Welcome to Seattle, and welcome to the Sasquatch. Great to see you."

"Thanks, I'm glad to be here," I say, matching his grin. "Plus, I'm already enjoying the cooler weather."

He chuckles. "Yeah, I can't say I'll miss Miami's humidity, although I'm told once the rains arrive, we'll be desperate for any scrap of sunshine we can find." He grins. "There's a reason the Twilight vampires were from around these parts." He gestures for me to follow him. "Come on in."

As he leads me through the office area, Coach Shaw's enthusiasm for the Sasquatch is clear. He inclines his head toward a large, glassed-in office where General Manager Carson Wells is sitting in a chair, deep in discussion with someone sitting across from him.

My gut tightens when I see who he's talking to. Rylan Collings. My new team captain sits rigid in his chair, his back straight and his shoulders tense. Even from here, the intensity rolls off him in waves.

A scene from last year flashes to my mind. It was late in the game when Seattle visited us. Collings was bearing down on me along the boards, all raw power and determination. He crushed me like a bug and then stripped the puck off me, smooth as silk, making me look like a rookie fresh out of juniors. My ribs still remember that monster check. I can't help grinning at the memory—when someone hands you your ass that cleanly, you've gotta respect the skill behind it.

Right now, though, there's something vulnerable about him. His jaw works back and forth as he listens to whatever the GM is saying.

Carson catches sight of Travis and me through the glass and waves us in. My heart rate kicks up a notch as we step into Wells' office.

Rylan's composed expression slips for a fraction of a second when I enter. He looks even more tense, if that's possible. But he recovers quickly, his game face sliding back into place as he stands.

"Jamie Pirelli, welcome." Carson Wells extends his hand, his grip firm and confident. He's one of the youngest General Managers in the NHL, maybe in his early forties, but there's an air of quiet authority to him, and he's well-respected around the league. "We weren't expecting you until tomorrow."

"I was able to get an earlier flight." My voice is steadier than I feel as I shake his hand.

Rylan Collings stands perfectly still; his expression is unreadable, but there's an undercurrent in the tense way he holds himself that makes my stomach clench.

It's not outright hostility, but it's not warmth either. His light brown hair is shorter than I remember from the last time I played opposite him, and there's a touch of premature gray at his temples. That shouldn't be hot, but somehow, it is.

"Hey, Rylan, good to see you again," I say, meeting his gaze directly, hoping I can diffuse whatever this tension is with some good, old-fashioned friendliness.

"You too, Pirelli."

We shake hands, and when our palms touch, it's like a jolt of electricity shoots up my arm. *Holy shit.* My breath catches in my throat as our eyes lock. Up close, his are an unusual mix of blue and gray, like storm clouds over the ocean.

He's taller than me by a couple of inches, and while I probably outweigh him by a few pounds, the way he carries himself, as if he's holding something back, makes him seem bigger.

Travis and Carson are talking, but their voices fade into the background as all my senses zero in on Rylan. The way his jaw clenches and unclenches. The steady rise and fall of his chest under his fitted grey Henley.

He shifts on his feet, and I swear to god, I can feel the air move between us. Every tiny movement he makes registers with me like a blip on a radar screen.

This is not good. Get it together, Pirelli. You're here to play hockey, not develop an inconvenient crush on your team captain.

But my body is *not* getting the memo, and liquid warmth pools in my lower belly. *Fuck me sideways.*

"Sorry, we don't want to interrupt," Travis says, but Carson waves him off. "No, it's fine. We were just finishing up here. I'm glad you two can officially meet before camp starts tomorrow. It's going to be an intense season. We all need to hit the ground running." He turns to Rylan.

"Thanks for meeting with me, Collings. We'll talk more later this week," he says, and Rylan nods.

"Of course. I'll see everyone tomorrow," he says with a polite smile before moving past me to the door. I catch a whiff of his cologne, something clean and woodsy. The hair on the back of my neck stands up as our shoulders brush on his way out.

Well. That was... something. My new captain obviously has some thoughts about my arrival, and I'm pretty sure none of them are good. The memory of his earlier vulnerable expression tugs at me, making me wonder what they were discussing before Travis and I walked in.

"Have a seat, Jamie." Carson gestures to the chair Rylan just vacated. "We have quite a bit to talk about."

"So, we believe you're going to fit in well here," he says after we've settled in our chairs. "I know Coach Shaw and his staff have some exciting plans for you."

Travis nods in agreement. "We've got a solid core group, and your speed and creativity are exactly what we need on our top line with Collings and Coté."

The knot in my stomach loosens a little.

"I appreciate the opportunity," I say, meaning every word. "I know there are... concerns about my... time with the Jaguars."

They both nod, their expressions serious. Carson looks at Coach Shaw, who leans forward, his elbows on his knees. "Look, Jamie, I watched you pretty closely while we worked in Florida together. I know how much talent you have, and I also know you've got a great work ethic. I know things in that locker room weren't ideal, especially for an LGBTQ player."

"That being said," Carson interjects, his tone gentle but firm, "we're taking a calculated risk here. The

Sasquatch team culture we're building is important. We believe in you, but you'll need to prove yourself to your teammates."

"Of course." I straighten in my chair. "Whatever it takes."

We talk for a few more minutes about how I'll fit into the lineup, and Coach's plans for how to use my skills. The familiar territory of hockey strategy settles my nerves. This is what I know, what I'm good at. It's nothing like Florida, where I was constantly fighting for ice time and trying to prove myself worthy of a roster spot.

"We're building something special here," Carson says. "There's an opportunity for you to be a big part of that. But it's really up to you, Jamie."

"I promise, I'm up for the challenge," I say confidently.

CHAPTER 3

RYLAN

I unlock my front door, stepping into the familiar calm of my apartment. The late afternoon sun streams through floor-to-ceiling windows of the impersonal but beautiful high-rise condo with peekaboo views of Elliott Bay. Everything sits exactly where it's supposed to in the open-concept space, throw pillows placed neatly on the charcoal sectional, coffee table magazines aligned at right angles, kitchen counters gleaming and uncluttered.

The familiarity of my space should calm me, but tonight it just feels empty. My brother Nick's OHL jersey hangs in its frame on the wall, the only personal touch in the whole place. Everything else could belong to anyone. The neutral gray and black colors, the clean surfaces and modern furniture chosen more for style than comfort.

Tossing my keys on the table, I toe off my shoes and set them on the rack by the door before heading down the hall. My housekeeper was here today and the fresh citrusy smell of cleaning products lingers in the air. My bedroom has the same minimalist feel as the rest of the place, my bed made and my closet perfectly organized.

Everything controlled. Everything in its place. No surprises, no mess, no chaos. This is the one space I can control just about every detail. Even though I've lived here for three years, my condo still looks like a show home. That's how I've always liked it.

A career spent bouncing between teams has taught me how to live with the knowledge that I could be traded at any time, meaning I'll have to pack up and move at the drop of a hat. The minimalism of my home is kind of like armor against that uncertainty. Usually, the rigid order helps my nerves in check, gives me something solid to hold on to. But right now, the pristine countertops and careful organization are not doing jack shit to calm the swarm of butterflies in my stomach. Between that loaded talk with Carson and running into Jamie fucking Pirelli, my carefully maintained equilibrium is shot to hell, and no amount of perfectly arranged throw pillows can fix that.

I change into comfortable grey sweatpants and a soft, well-worn t-shirt from my junior days. I need to find a calmer headspace. With camp starting tomorrow morning, I can't afford distractions, especially with what I now know about the owners being *this close* to blowing up the whole team.

Unfortunately, the soothing predictability of my weekly meal prep routine doesn't work to settle me this evening. My mind keeps drifting back to the moment Jamie Pirelli walked into Carson's office. Those blue eyes, the unexpected jolt that shot through my entire body when we shook hands. His presence hit me like a physical force—and that is not something I want to examine right now.

The knife slips as I'm dicing chicken, almost catching my finger. "Fuck." I set it down, bracing both hands against the counter. I cannot afford to lose my shit now. Not with the team in such a precarious position. Not with everything I've worked so goddamn hard to keep buried.

My throat tightens. Thirteen years in the NHL, keeping this part of myself locked up so tight that sometimes I can almost pretend it doesn't exist. But five minutes in the same room as Jamie Pirelli and suddenly it's like my walls are made of glass instead of brick.

The opening notes of "The Hockey Song" blast from my phone, and relief floods through me at the familiar tune. *Thank fuck.* I grab it like a drowning man reaching for a life preserver.

"Hey, Lou."

"Dude! You'll never believe what just happened to me at Whole Foods. So this chick comes over to me, right, and—"

He stops mid-sentence—like somehow he can tell, before I've even said one damn word that something's going on. We've been close for so long, that Lou knows what I'm feeling before I do a lot of the time. He knows almost everything about me. With one very large exception.

"What's going on?" he asks.

"Nothing. Just... you know... getting ready for camp tomorrow." Despite my best efforts, my voice is strained.

"Ry." His tone shifts. "You've done, like, a dozen training camps. Try again."

I lean against the counter, pinching the bridge of my nose and squeezing my eyes shut. *Resistance is use-*

less, I swear. "Carson told me today that the Ever-tons aren't happy," I say, referring to the wealthy family who owns the Sasquatch. "They're leaning on Carson to produce significantly better results by the All-Star break or..." I trail off, not wanting to say it out loud.

"Yeah? What else?"

"What else? That's not enough?"

"That's not what's got you so worked up. I know you." His voice is gentle. Lou and I have been best friends since we were little kids playing shinny on frozen ponds. He knew me before Nick and my mom died. Before my dad started drink-ing and everything changed. So he's seen me spiral plenty of times. He can handle it.

I sigh. "I'm fine. Just tired. Got a lot on my mind with losing Freeman and Coulson, and these new guys coming in."

"Mhmm." He doesn't push, though I can tell he wants to.

"What do you think about the Pirelli thing?"

My stomach clenches. "He's talented."

"Yeah, but that's not what I mean. You think the guys will give him shit about being bi?"

I grip the phone tighter. "I hope not. We've got good guys in our room. I think most of them are open-minded. And anyone who has a problem with it knows better than to say anything. Or at least they should." My tone is sharp.

"True. What about the shit that went down with Belov?"

"That's..." I sigh. "I don't know. It's hard to know what's true."

"I heard Belov was a real prick to him." Lou's voice darkens. "Stupid, old-school mentality about him being bi, or whatever. Making stupid comments about Pirelli checking them out in the showers and having HIV or some fucked up bullshit. It's fuckin' ridiculous in this day and age."

"Yeah." My voice is rough. I clear my throat. "As long as he shows up and plays hard, I'll make sure the team falls in line, but I don't think we have anyone who will be an asshole about it. If Pirelli can do what Travis Shaw thinks he can, he'll be a big help. And we fucking need that. We don't have a lot of time to make ownership happy."

"Yeah. We'll make it happen, though. Just gotta believe, Ry. We got this." Lou's an eternal optimist.

"I fucking hope so."

After hanging up with Lou, I head to my bedroom. My laptop sits waiting for me like some kind of silent challenge.

My fingers hover over the keyboard before I type his name. *What am I even doing?* I don't Google-stalk my teammates. I don't obsess. But there's something about him... something different.

The first articles are straightforward: "First Openly Bisexual Player Drafted to NHL." There's a photo of him at eighteen, all golden curls and that infectious grin. Draft day. His parents are beaming beside him as he dons the Florida Jaguars jersey. A picture of pure potential.

I scroll down on the page. Charity work. LGBTQ youth support. Interviews where he speaks about representation with honest intelligence that makes me weirdly uncomfortable. Not because of what he's saying. But because I recognize something in him. Like he knows what it feels like to be an outsider.

Sounds familiar.

The media narrative shifts late in his first year. "Jaguars' Pirelli Spotted at Club Before Big Game." There are photos of him stumbling out of various South Beach nightclubs at dawn, with rosy cheeks and messy hair, his clothes rumpled. "Jamie Pirelli Linked to Reality Star." My chest tightens.

I want to stop scrolling, but I can't help myself. Stories and tweets about missed practices and public fights with teammates. The golden boy who went off the rails, acting out all over Miami's club scene.

"Party Boy Pirelli's Wild Night Out" is the headline on one gossip site, and my mouth goes dry as the image fills my screen.

Jamie's sandwiched between a man and a woman as they stumble out of some club in South Beach. The woman's dress is microscopic, her tanned skin and curves spilling out everywhere. The guy is all sharp angles and designer jeans. But Jamie... I swallow hard. His shirt hangs open, revealing perfectly carved abs, shiny with sweat. His golden curls are wild, like someone's been running their fingers through them. His face is flushed, his blue eyes glazed, and that mouth is curved into a lazy, satisfied smile that sends a rush of heat straight to my cock. Jealousy burns acid-hot in my throat.

He looks freshly fucked. And the sight makes me goddamn crazy.

"Fuck," I growl, slamming the laptop closed.

My room is suddenly too hot. Too small. My shorts are uncomfortably tight, and I'm hard as steel just from a fucking photo.

This is a problem. I've spent thirteen years in the NHL keeping this part of myself locked down tight. I don't take risks. No chances of being exposed. Nothing that could crack the perfect facade of Captain Rylan Collings.

I force myself out of bed and stomp into the bathroom, where I splash cold water on my face. The guy staring back at me from the mirror looks haunted: shadows under his eyes, his jaw clenched.

I strip and step into the shower, cranking the water as cold as it'll go. The icy spray hits my skin like needles, but it does nothing to calm the heat coursing through my veins. My cock is still half-hard, the traitorous fucker.

I try to think about plays, about defensive coverage, about anything except Jamie Pirelli, but that stupid image won't leave my mind. Those blue eyes. That mouth. He's the picture of a man who knows exactly what he wants... and exactly how to get it.

As if I'm unable to stop it, my hand slides down my abs. The images of Pirelli's perfectly carved muscles, his skin shining with sweat, are seared into my brain.

"Fuck," I groan, wrapping my fingers around my cock.

I stroke myself faster, hating myself for it, but powerless to stop as I imagine him pushing me up against the shower wall, feeling the heat of his skin against mine.

This isn't a choice anymore. This is pure need.

My heavy breaths echo off the tiles as I picture how he would look at me if I dropped to my knees in front of him. Ready to worship at the altar of his perfect body. I can almost hear the sounds he would make when I'd swallow him down. The way he would thread those fingers through my hair and hold my head in position. Taking everything he wanted from me.

The water pounds against my back as I chase my release, lost in my fantasy. Jamie moaning my name.

His hands on my body. His mouth on mine, hot and demanding.

"Fuuuuck," I groan, and then I'm coming hard, pleasure spiking through me as I spill over my fist. For a moment, my vision whites out, all that tension releasing in one desperate rush.

Reality crashes back as the evidence disappears down the drain. Shame burns in my gut, my cheeks flaming. *What the fuck am I doing? Jesus fucking Christ.*

I shut off the water, drying myself quickly and pulling on fresh boxers and a t-shirt while carefully avoiding looking at myself in the mirror. I set my phone face-down on the nightstand before sliding back into my bed.

Tomorrow I'll be the team captain again, focused only on hockey and leadership. I'll welcome Pirelli professionally, help him settle in, and maintain appropriate boundaries.

Maybe if I keep telling myself that, I'll believe it. But as I lie in bed, I can't help but wonder what it would be like to allow myself to *really* want someone. To let myself experience that kind of desire without the constant, overwhelming fear of losing everything I've worked for.

I don't know if I'll ever be brave enough to find out.

CHAPTER 4

JAMIE

The Sasquatch's high-tech meeting room screams money and professionalism, way more impressive than anything we had in Florida. My sneakers barely make a sound on the carpeted floor as I slip into a seat near the middle, not too close to the front like an eager rookie, but not hiding in the back, either. Being fifteen minutes early probably makes me look like an ass-kisser, but it's better than being late and making a bad first impression. My leg bounces under the built-in desktop as I try to appear casual.

The first few guys filter in a few minutes later. A tall, dark-haired guy, a defenseman I think, drops into a seat near the front, immediately getting into a conversation with a redheaded guy with a British accent about some Netflix show. Their comfortable back-and-forth, complete with inside jokes, reinforces my status as the outsider in the room.

More players arrive in small groups, and the room slowly fills with the boisterous energy that comes from reuniting after the off-season, with guys comparing summer tans and sharing vacation stories. I recognize a lot of the faces from having played against them, but not everyone.

A few curious glances are thrown my way, along with some polite nods, but no one approaches me. I get it. I'm the dude with the asshole reputation, and no one's sure it was smart to bring me onto this already struggling team. I'm aware of the whispers, but I keep an easy smile on my face. If the last three seasons have taught me anything, it's 'never let 'em see you sweat'.

Louis Tremblay, the starting goalie, walks in with his signature grin. I know he and Rylan Collings are tight. I think they grew up together in some small town in Canada.

Tanner Sinclair, my fellow trade acquisition, arrives next, looking as uncertain as I feel. We exchange quick nods, but he sits down next to Lou. Makes sense, I guess, wanting to sit next to the other goaltender. It's not like we knew each other well in Florida since he was on the farm team. Even so, the knot in my stomach twists at the feeling of rejection.

I make a conscious effort to stop drumming my fingers on the desktop. First impressions matter, and I'm hyper-aware of every move I make; I know I'm being watched. But after the mess of my last three years, I *cannot* screw up this chance. It could be my last one in the league.

Coach Shaw and GM Carson Wells walk in together, their presence shifting the room's energy, conversations immediately dying down. Rylan slips in behind them, moving to a chair in the front row with quiet confidence.

The GM clears his throat, drawing everyone's attention. "Welcome back, gentlemen. It's great to see all your faces again, and some new ones, too." He nods in my direction, and I sit up a little straighter.

"We've got a big season ahead of us. The last couple of years have been disappointing, but we're putting that behind us right now. This is a new beginning, a chance to start fresh."

Murmurs of agreement come from around the room. I glance at Rylan again, but his eyes are fixed on Carson, his expression unreadable.

"Part of that fresh start is bringing in some new blood, both on the ice and off. As you're all aware by now, we made a significant move at the last minute." More noises of acknowledgment follow, and a few guys send looks my way.

"I understand this kind of change isn't always easy. We'll miss the guys who've moved on, but I truly believe we've put together a group that can do something special this year. So I want to take a couple of minutes to introduce our newest teammates."

He introduces all the new guys, starting with the rookies, and everyone stands up and says a quick hello until he gets to me.

"And last but not least, joining us from the Florida Jaguars is forward Jamie Pirelli."

I stand, forcing a smile onto my face. My palms are sweaty as I nod at my new teammates.

"Thanks, guys. I'm excited to be part of this team. Can't wait to see what we'll do this season," I say before sinking back into my seat. Yeah, that was lame, but no one expects a huge speech. The only way I'm going to earn anyone's respect is with my actions. Nothing I say at some stupid welcome meeting will count for shit if I don't perform.

Carson introduces Coach Shaw next, who steps forward with a friendly smile on his face. Even with his open expression, his presence commands the room. He's not a huge guy, but he's solidly built with thick, gray hair and steely blue eyes that look like they cut through bullshit like a hot knife through butter. He has that rare combination of natural authority and approachability that the best coaches have.

Shaw is a former player, but he was more of a journeyman than a star. He was the kind of player known for always having his teammates' backs. He's been coaching in the farm system for a few years, but this is his first head coaching job at this level, so I'm sure he's feeling the pressure as much as we are.

"Thanks, Carson," he says in that voice that makes you sit up and pay attention. Commanding without being intimidating.

"The past couple of seasons have been tough on everyone in this room," he continues. "But that's behind us. We're going to focus on the present, on putting in the work every single day to get back to where we all want to be."

There are nods and murmurs of agreement from around the room. I find myself nodding along, feeling the spark of excitement that I've been missing for the past couple of years.

Sometimes, I still can't believe I get paid to do what most kids only dream about. During all the toxic locker room drama with the Jags, I kind of forgot how much I truly love playing hockey. Maybe his trade means more than just a chance to save my reputation—maybe it's what I need to reconnect with the game. To find the pure thrill that used to hit me every time I stepped out on the ice.

"The talent in this room is incredible," he continues. "But talent alone doesn't win championships. It takes hard work, dedication, and most importantly, it takes coming together as a team. And the responsibility for that falls equally on all our shoulders."

It could be my imagination, but I feel like he looks at me when he says it. I swallow hard, sitting up a little straighter.

"The coaching staff has spent the last couple of weeks laying out some tentative game plans for next week, which we'll be covering during practices, but there is one off-ice change that I want to bring up right now." He pauses as everyone's ears perk up.

"All players, regardless of the number of years in the league, will be sharing a room with a teammate while we're on the road this year."

RYLAN

The coffee I'm drinking takes a wrong turn when Coach Shaw drops the bomb about the new roommate policy. I fight to mask the sudden, choking sound I make as a simple cough, but it doesn't fly. Louis gives me a worried glance, but I refuse to meet his eyes, concentrating on keeping a straight face as surprised whispers spread through the room.

Sharing rooms isn't the norm anymore, especially for veterans. Anyone who's not on their entry-level contract gets their own room. It's an unwritten rule, part of "making it" in the league.

"I'm aware this is a bit unorthodox," Travis continues, "But I'm a firm believer that building strong bonds off the ice translates to success on the ice. We're going to get to know each other better than we know our own families this year."

Through my peripheral vision, I catch Jamie Pirelli shifting in his seat, his casual posture betrayed by the way his fingers drum nervously against his thigh. But his expression is composed, an easy half-smile playing at his lips.

Travis must sense the room's uneasiness because he holds up a placating hand. "Look, I understand it's going to be an adjustment, but I've put a lot of thought into the roommate pairings. When I met with each of you during the off-season, I tried to get a sense of who you are as people, not just as players. My goal is to facilitate connections between all of us. I'm not looking to force anyone into an uncomfortable situation. If anyone has a serious problem with sharing a room, you can come speak to me privately, but my hope is that you'll give this a real shot."

He gives us a grin before continuing. "And just to show you how invested the coaching staff is in this idea, we'll all be sharing rooms this year too." That's met with some laughter, and a few of the assistant coaches roll their eyes in an exaggerated fashion, which breaks some of the tension.

"Okay, so before the speculation gets too out of hand, I'm going to go ahead and tell you who you're rooming with this year," Coach Shaw grins as he pulls out a sheet of paper and puts on his reading glasses.

My stomach clenches as he starts reading names. "Marshall with Darbyshire. Reese-McLeod and Gagnon." Some guys fist-bump while others maintain their professional masks as Coach goes down the list.

"Sinclair with Tremblay." Louis shoots his new backup an encouraging smile.

"Collings with Pirelli."

The words hit me like a blind check. Austin sucks in a sharp breath behind me, but I'm still trying to control the rushing sound of blood in my ears. Oh my god, he's not just my teammate—I jerked off to thoughts of my *roommate* less than 12 hours ago.

Fuck. My. Life.

Okay, get it together, Collings. I need to set the example here and show everyone this isn't a big deal.

Even if the thought of sharing a room with Jamie Pirelli makes my heart race in a way that has nothing to do with hockey.

Chapter 5

Rylan

The locker room buzzes with energy as we gear up for our first on-ice practice of the year. I deliberately focus on my own stall, going through my familiar routine and putting on each piece of equipment in the exact same order I've used since I was a kid. Pirelli's been assigned the stall two down from mine. Close enough that I keep catching hints of his cologne mixed with coffee when he moves past me.

Austin, on my other side, is quiet and broody, as usual. But there's something pointed in the way he positions himself, almost like he's trying to create a buffer between Jamie and me. I'm not sure what that's about, but I'm grateful, anyway. It keeps Pirelli mostly out of my line of sight, and honestly, I don't need the distraction.

I hit the ice first, as usual. The rink's familiar scent fills my lungs, as comforting as a warm blanket on a chilly day. The cool, crisp air mingles with the sharp tang of the ice, and it quiets the noise in my head just a little as I breathe it in.

This is home. It's been home for as long as I can remember. An image of Nick flashes through my mind, his grin wide as he flies past me, heading for the goal. The rink is always where I've come to work out whatever's on my mind. After Nick died, our town's rink manager, Jerry, used to let me skate late at night after everyone else had gone home. Sometimes until two or three in the morning, just skating and shooting puck after puck into the empty net until my legs nearly gave out.

Even now, I still feel Nick with me every time I step onto the ice. Hockey was the bond my brother and I shared, the thread that wove our lives together. It's *still* what holds me together. I wouldn't know who I am without hockey. It's the bedrock I've built my life on.

I take a few laps before the rest of the guys start making their way out. When Jamie comes on, he hops onto the ice and accelerates away with the confidence that comes from a lifetime of being the best player out here. He hasn't put his helmet on yet, and his shaggy blond curls blow back off his face as he rounds the first curve. He's an incredible skater, fast and graceful, each stride deliberate and powerful as he moves across the surface.

He looks just like Nick.

That thought almost knocks the breath out of my lungs, and my stride falters. But Coach's whistle saves me from dwelling on it.

We take a few minutes to stretch before separating into three groups for some simple drills, the kind we've all been doing since we were kids. Of course, Jamie and I get grouped together, along with Austin, the rookie, Olivier Gagnon, and a couple of other guys.

Jamie starts off, his movements fluid and precise as he weaves through the cones. Each turn is sharp, showcasing his natural agility. His cheeks are flushed pink from the cold and the exercise, and his blue eyes sparkle with joy. It's easy to see how much he loves this. Most guys see practice as a necessary evil, a boring chore we all have to do before getting to the good stuff: the game. But Jamie seems to love every second of it, even the drudgery.

Louis skates up beside me during a break in the drills. "Kid's got moves," he says with a grin before tilting his head back to squirt water into his mouth.

"Yeah," I reply, trying to sound nonchalant.

We move into a short scrimmage, and as expected, Coach has Jamie and me together on the top line with Austin. One of the guys who got shipped to Florida rounded out our top line last year, so it's no surprise that Jamie's taking his place.

What is surprising is how natural it feels. Jamie's ability to read plays and anticipate movements is uncanny. They say some players have an innate hockey sense, a weird ability to see how the game is going to play out and react to things almost before they happen. It's not the kind of thing you can teach. Nick had it, and obviously, Jamie does too. When I send a no-look pass across the ice, he's right there to receive it, like we've been playing together for years instead of minutes. We have the kind of chemistry that can't be manufactured, no matter how many drills you run.

Meanwhile, Austin plays with an edge I haven't seen for a while. He's not being overtly aggressive with Jamie, but there's a coldness to his interactions. When Jamie calls for the puck, Austin hesitates a fraction too long before passing. The timing is off just enough that Jamie has to adjust his speed, which throws off what should have been a perfect setup.

Pirelli just gives a slight nod and keeps playing, but I catch the way his jaw tightens.

The next time he gets open, Austin straight-up ignores him, choosing instead to take a worse shot that Louis blocks easily. Jamie's in perfect position for the rebound, but Austin swoops in and claims it instead, circling back around to reset the play.

Coach Shaw watches intently, his expression unreadable, until he blows the whistle to signal the end of practice.

"Good work today, gentlemen." His gaze sweeps over all of us but lingers on Austin for a moment longer than usual. "Generally, I like what I'm seeing, but we have plenty of work to do. Tomorrow afternoon's skate is open to season ticket holders, so everyone needs to bring their A-game and their smiles."

As we file off the ice, Coach skates up beside Austin. "Coté, I need a word before you head out. Come by my office after you shower."

"Of course," Austin replies, but there's tension in his voice.

I'm the only one who overhears their conversation, but I act like I didn't hear a thing. Austin stays silent as we enter the locker room, but my guess is Coach is going to want an explanation for Austin's attitude toward Pirelli. I'm just as curious, but it's not something I'll mention unless it becomes a bigger problem.

As the guys disperse—some to the trainers, others to the weight room or the showers, I hang back. I need a minute to breathe, to process the whirlwind of emotions stirred up by watching Jamie Pirelli play hockey like he's the reincarnation of my older brother. My older brother who's been dead for almost twenty years.

It's not just the similarity to Nick, though that's part of it. It's the way he brings out something in my own game I'd nearly forgotten was there. Something that feels strangely thrilling and terrifyingly close to joy.

CHAPTER 6

RYLAN

The practice facility is packed, every seat filled with season ticket holders eager to get their first look at this year's team. Even the standing-room areas are crowded with fans, their phones out and ready to document every moment. The energy in the building reminds me of our championship season, full of hope and expectation.

I hate it.

Give me an empty rink any day with only the sound of blades on the ice, the thunk of pucks against boards, and the familiar rhythm of drills. But this circus of forced smiles and small talk? This is more like my own, personal version of hell.

"Look alive, Captain." Louis bumps my shoulder as we make our way onto the ice. "Your face is doing that thing again."

"What thing?"

"That 'I'd rather be getting a root canal' thing." He grins, somehow already in performance mode. Lou's always been good at this part—the showmanship, the connecting with fans. Me, not so much.

I force my features into something resembling a smile, but Louis shakes his head. "Maybe dial it back a notch. You've got a bit of a deranged serial killer look going on."

Before I can respond, a wave of cheers erupts from the crowd as Jamie Pirelli steps onto the ice, his whole face lighting up as he acknowledges the fans. He flips a puck over the glass to a kid in a Sasquatch jersey, and one of the local network's cameras swings to capture the moment.

"He's good at this," Louis observes.

I grunt in response, trying to focus on my warm-up stretches. But my eyes keep drifting back to Pirelli.

Nick used to thrive on stuff like this, too. He was such an amazing talent that he had other kids coming to watch him play hockey by the time he was thirteen years old. I push the memory away and focus on Coach Shaw as he calls us to center ice.

"Alright, gentleman," Travis says, his voice pitched low enough that the media can't pick it up. "Let's show 'em what Sasquatch hockey looks like."

We break into drill groups, and I try to lose myself in the familiar rhythm of practice, but it's impossible to forget about the audience. Every time Jamie touches the puck, a ripple of excitement moves through the crowd. When he and I connect on a particularly nice pass, the cheers are immediate. The media people are leaning forward, their cameras capturing everything.

"Looking good, boys!" Charlie calls after we score a beautiful goal on Louis. Jamie grins and raises his stick in a subtle acknowledgment to the fans who are cheering. It's kind of a perfect gesture: he connects with the crowd, but he doesn't disrupt practice. He's clearly a natural at this kind of stuff. Yet another thing he has in common with my older brother.

"Collings." Coach Shaw's voice snaps me back to reality. "Run that power play setup again."

I nod, grateful for something else to focus on. This is what I'm good at: the technical aspects of hockey, the precise execution of plays. Pirelli can handle the showmanship.

As we work through the drills, it's impossible not to see the way he elevates everyone around him. He's got Olivier Gagnon looking more confident already, setting up perfect one-timers for the rookie. The kid's practically glowing under the positive attention.

"Pirelli's got good instincts," Louis says during a water break, jerking his chin toward Jamie. "And not only with the puck."

He's right. Jamie seems to know exactly when to push the pace and when to dial it back. When to play it straight, and when to add a little flair for the fans. Even Austin's starting to thaw, especially after Jamie sets him up for a booming slap shot that draws appreciative gasps from the crowd.

"Okay, we're going to wrap this up with some three-on-three," Coach calls. "Show them some real hockey."

As we line up for the scrimmage, Pirelli catches my eye. He's got a look on his face that makes my stomach flip. "Ready to give them a show, Cap?"

I should say something professional about focusing on execution. Instead, I find myself caught in his gaze like a fly caught in a spider's web. The only difference is that I'm not sure I want to fight my way out of it.

When the scrimmage starts, everything else fades away. There's just the ice, the puck, and the impossible way Jamie Pirelli anticipates my every move. We're scoring on Lou almost at will, connecting on plays that shouldn't be possible for two players who've only been linemates for a few hours.

When Coach blows the whistle to end practice, the crowd erupts in genuine excitement. Jamie raises his stick to them again, that million-dollar smile lighting up his whole face. The cameras are eating it up, and I can hear the reporters already starting their commentary about our "explosive chemistry" on the ice.

"Good show, boys," Travis says as we gather one last time. "Hit the showers, then stick around for autographs and meet and greets. The PR team has everything set up in the lobby."

Jamie's already moving toward the boards, tossing more pucks to kids as he skates past. Every gesture looks genuine and unforced. Natural as breathing.

"Coming, Cap?" Louis asks, waiting at the bench.

I nod, squaring my shoulders. Time to put on the public face and be the leader everyone expects. But as I follow my team into the locker room, I can't shake the feeling that Jamie Pirelli is about to complicate my life in ways that have nothing to do with hockey.

JAMIE

Most of the guys head right into the showers, but I take my time removing my gear. My hands are shaky as I unlace my skates, the post-practice high already fading as I think about the media scrum waiting for us.

In Florida, I learned the hard way that reporters aren't your friends. Fans are one thing, but reporters are vipers. No matter how casual they act, how much they smile and joke and act like they're your friend, they're always looking for an angle. And I've given them plenty of ammunition over the years.

Riley from the PR department pokes her head into the room. "Hey, Pirelli? Media wants to talk to you and Collings about your chemistry out there today."

"Great." I try to keep the sarcasm out of my voice. Riley's just doing her job.

"Don't worry," she adds with a kind smile. "Rylan's great with them. Follow his lead."

Speaking of our captain, he's ready to go, of course, dressed in his Sasquatch-branded workout gear. He looks more at ease than I've seen him all day. Not like he's about to walk into a nest of snipers.

"Ready?" he asks, stopping in front of my stall.

Not even close. But I nod, jamming my forest green Sasquatch ball cap on backward over my wet hair. It probably makes me look like some kind of punk kid, but whatever.

The media room is packed with way more reporters than I expected for a simple practice. Everyone wants their pound of flesh.

Rylan takes the center seat at the table with practiced ease. I settle beside him, trying to resist the urge to hide behind him. Both literally and figuratively.

"We'll start with local media," Jared Dawson, the team's PR manager, calls out, and the questions begin.

"Collings," someone calls out. "The team looked great today. How much of that is because of the new additions?"

"We're excited about the energy all our new players bring. Pirelli, in particular, has a creative playing style that complements our system well. But camp only started yesterday, so we've got a lot of work ahead of us."

His answer is perfect: professional, inclusive, and measured. No headline-grabbing quotes, nothing that could be twisted out of context.

"Jamie." A sharp-featured woman in the front row fixes me with a predatory smile. "Your departure from Florida was... controversial. Any response to Vladimir Belov's recent comments about team chemistry?"

My stomach churns. Of course, they're bringing up Belov. That asshole got under my skin so badly that we ended up brawling in the locker room at the end of last season. The final straw? His disgusting "jokes" about me being HIV positive and leaving an at-home test kit in my stall. I don't believe being HIV positive is anything to be ashamed of, but it sure as fuck isn't a joke.

No surprise to anyone, the Jags PR team stayed quiet about the incident, allowing the media to invent their own stories of what caused the fight. Given my history, it was easy for them to make it all my fault in the court of public opinion. Earlier this week he tweeted something shitty about how much better

Jaguars were "clicking" since the departure of certain former players, obviously targeted directly at me.

Anger flares in my chest. My mouth opens, a sarcastic retort about Belov's own questionable "chemistry" with certain cocktail waitresses right on the tip of my tongue. It would feel *so* good to throw that hypocritical asshole under the bus.

But Rylan cuts in smoothly before I can speak.

"We're focused on moving forward," he says firmly. "Jamie's our teammate now, and he's already showing why our management was so eager to bring him to Seattle."

The tension drains from my shoulders as I realize what almost happened. One snippy comment, and there'd be headlines about me being a bitter, vindictive ex-teammate. *Fuck.*

The reporter tries again. "But surely the concerns about—"

"Like I said," Rylan interrupts, his tone pleasant but inviting no argument, "we're looking forward, not back. Next question?"

I shoot him a grateful look. He gives me the briefest nod, so subtle that I doubt anyone else notices, but it settles something in my chest. He has my back with the media... Like a team captain is supposed to... *Huh. That's a pleasant change.*

The questions continue about easier things like our new line combinations and other expectations for the season. Rylan handles most of them, and his answers are consistently thoughtful but never reveal anything of substance. It's like watching a master class in media management.

"Jamie," another reporter calls out. "You and Rylan showed some serious chemistry during the scrimmage. Did you expect to click so fast with your new captain?"

This one I can handle. "Honestly? No. That kind of connection normally takes more time to develop. But Rylan's a great player, it makes it easy to read off him. The whole team's been very welcoming."

A different reporter tries to bait me again, but I'm ready for it this time. "Jamie, how does it feel being in a more progressive locker room?"

"It's great. Like I said, the whole team has been very welcoming."

But this reporter isn't done. "My next question is for Team Captain Collings: Since Pirelli joined the

Sasquatch, has anyone expressed concerns about sharing facilities with—"

"We are done with that line of questioning." Rylan's voice cuts through the room like ice. His expression hasn't changed, but there's steel in his tone. "This organization judges players on their hockey skills and their moral character, nothing else. Next?"

The rest of the media session passes in a blur. I focus on breathing, on keeping my expression neutral, and on not giving them anything they can use against me or the team. Rylan continues fielding most questions, occasionally setting me up for safe responses about hockey-specific topics.

Finally, Jared calls time. As chairs scrape and reporters pack up their gear, I keep my ass parked, not quite trusting my legs yet. My hands are still trembling from the adrenaline of nearly fucking up again.

"You okay?" Rylan asks quietly, leaning closer so the lingering reporters can't hear.

"Yeah." I manage a weak smile, looking up to meet his concerned gaze. "Thanks for the assist back there. I was about to open my mouth and make a nasty comment without thinking. You saved me from myself."

"That's what teammates do." His voice is soft, almost gentle, and something in his expression makes my breath catch. Our eyes lock, and that same electric current from the ice crackles between us. He looks away first, a flush creeping up his neck.

"The vultures are mostly gone," Charlie announces, poking his head in. "Coast is clear if you want to head out."

But Rylan's already moving toward the door. "Come on, Pirelli," he calls over his shoulder.

I haul my ass out of my chair and follow Rylan and Charlie into the locker room. I'm relieved that Rylan was there to prevent me from screwing up, but I'm also pretty damn dejected. Even now, in a new city with a supposedly fresh start, everyone is still trying to define me by my sexuality first, my hockey second. It's depressing as fuck.

After gathering our stuff, the three of us head toward the players' exit when a tentative voice calls out, "Um, excuse me? Jamie Pirelli?"

I turn to find a teenager, maybe thirteen or fourteen, clutching a Sasquatch jersey from last season's Pride Night. The white fabric is covered in rainbow and trans pride pins, and there's a bisexual pride flag patch carefully sewn onto one shoulder.

"Hey." My smile is genuine this time. Talking to young fans, especially queer kids, always gives me a boost.

"I just..." The kid twists the jersey between nervous fingers. "I wanted to say thank you. For being out. It's so awesome to have a queer player on the Sasquatch! It means a lot to kids like me."

Beside me, Rylan goes still.

"Thanks for telling me. I really appreciate it." I reach for the jersey. "Want me to sign this?"

The kid's face lights up. "That would be amazing!"

While I'm signing, they tell me about playing for their local community team and how their teammates have been surprisingly cool since they came out as non-binary last year. "My captain and our coach have been awesome. They shut down anyone who tried to give me crap."

"Sounds like you've got some good leadership on your team," I say, glancing at Rylan, who's watching the interaction with an unreadable expression.

"The best." They clutch the signed jersey to their chest. "Thank you so much!"

After they leave, Rylan, Charlie, and I walk toward the parking lot. "That was brilliant," Charlie says, his green eyes wide. "Does that happen often?"

"More than you'd think," I reply to Charlie while trying to read Rylan's expression. He's still silent. "It's the best part of being out."

"Cool," Charlie responds. "Right, my car's over there, and I've gotta get home to let the new puppy out. Sandy's gonna murder my ass if that dog pisses on the carpet again. I'll catch you tomorrow, mates." He peels off toward his car, leaving Rylan and me.

Rylan's still silent, like he's deep in thought. "That must feel good. Talking to kids like that," he says thoughtfully.

"Yeah, it does," I say. "It's easy to focus on the shitty parts of being an out athlete, but most people don't think about the positive impact it makes on kids like that." I bump his shoulder gently with mine as we reach our cars. "Plus, it feels fucking awesome when they tell you how much it means to them."

His eyes meet mine for a brief moment before he looks away. "Yeah," he says softly.

"You good?" I ask, suddenly picking up on a strange vibe.

He shakes his head and looks around like he's trying to reorient himself or something.

"Yeah, I'm fine. I'll catch you tomorrow," he says, and we each get into our cars.

I pull out first, and when I glance in my rearview mirror, he's sitting in his driver's seat, watching me, his expression thoughtful.

CHAPTER 7

JAMIE

The team bus pulls up to our San Diego hotel just as the sun is setting. Even though it's late September, the air is warm, and the sky is slowly turning a deep velvety blue, with the stars just beginning to peek out. But even with the gorgeous surroundings, my gut is churning. It's our first road trip of the preseason, and my nerves aren't from the game—I can handle a preseason game without nerves. No, the swarm of butterflies in my tummy is because tonight I'll be sleeping only a couple of feet away from Rylan.

Charlie spent the ride from the airport rambling on about the restaurant in Little Italy he picked for the team dinner, but I barely registered a word, because I was way too focused on our captain, sitting a few rows ahead of us.

He spent the entire flight poring over his game notes like he was prepping for the SATs. He set up a workstation Martha Stewart would be proud of: about seventeen different highlighters with color-coordinat-ed post-it notes, and everything arranged in perfect right-angles to each other.

Honestly, it was kind of impressive. Almost as im-pressive as discovering just how far the Sasquatch ownership goes to make sure we're comfortable. The team's jet is in a totally different ballpark from what I'm used to from the Jaguars. It's outfitted with plush leather seats that fully recline, perfect for actually get-ting a decent rest. They also turn into legit worksta-tions if you need to focus, and there are sections with seats clustered around tables, so we can play cards or whatever. It was most definitely not a bad surprise.

The hotel lobby feels too warm as we file in for check-in. Veterans check in and pick up their keys first, but since my roommate happens to be the cap-tain, I don't have to wait with the younger guys. Rylan steps toward me, holding out my key card, his posture military-straight. "Here." He shoves it at me without meeting my eyes.

"Thanks, Cap." I make sure our fingers don't brush, but the air between us seems charged, anyway.

Austin's watching us with his jaw clenched. His eyes narrow before his expression shutters.

"Bets on which roommate pair will end up in a pillow fight first?" Charlie pipes up. "My money's on Tremblay and Sinclair!"

A few chuckles ripple through the group. I raise my arms and do a stupid little dance as Rylan and I walk away. "Later, suckas! The Cap and I will just have ourselves a nice nap while y'all are waiting in line for your keys!" I taunt.

A few guys snort at my antics, and a couple of others flip me the bird, so I'm laughing when Rylan and I step onto the elevator. We take our places in opposite corners, but for some reason, it feels impossibly, ridiculously small in here. "What floor?" I ask.

"Twelve," he replies with a tight smile.

I hit the button, and the silence stretches between us. Then, for some unexplained reason, the elevator glides smoothly to a stop. Halfway between the sixth and seventh floors.

"Hmm. Well, shit," he murmurs. "This is weird."

He makes a move toward the emergency phone thing in the corner just as the lights flicker.

Oh, fuck.

My entire body jumps into high alert. Getting trapped in an elevator ranks right at the top of my list of terrifying things.

My pulse thunders in my chest, my heart rate ramping up. I suck in a sharp breath, and Rylan's scent hits me. It's something crisp and woodsy. Reminds me of cedar trees.

Jesus, why am I focusing on how he smells right now? Probably because it's intoxicating. It makes me want to tear his clothes off right here in this tiny metal box.

Okay, so I might be panicking just a little. Are the walls closing in on us? Shit.

Then, with no warning, we start moving again, heading toward the 12th floor like nothing happened.

Rylan blows out a long breath.

Moments later we reach our floor without any more delays, although my heart's still racing.

"Are you okay?" He asks, looking at me suspiciously. "You look pale."

I swallow hard. "Yeah, I'm okay. Not a big fan of being trapped in the elevator."

Once in our room, Rylan starts unpacking right away, placing everything in his bag neatly into drawers and closets. I dump my stuff onto the other bed, deliberately letting my jacket fall half off the edge.

"You could use a hanger," he says, voice carefully neutral.

"Could," I agree, watching him try not to cringe as I kick off my shoes in different directions. "But I'm traumatized. I need to meditate or something."

I'm joking, but now that I said it, it doesn't sound like a bad idea.

He opens his mouth, closes it, and then heads for the door. "I'm going to grab some ice."

As soon as the door clicks shut behind him, I collapse onto my bed, running my hands through my hair. All I can think about is how good he smells, and how much I want to mess up his perfect composure.

It's probably just the adrenaline rush from our close call in the elevator, but I feel a little unhinged right now.

Fuck. This is going to be harder than I thought.

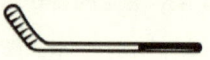

RYLAN

The ice bucket is weirdly heavy in my hands. I've been standing in this stupid hallway for the last two minutes, staring at the door of our room like the number might somehow change if I wait long enough.

Get it together, Collings.

My phone buzzes with a text from Louis.

Dinner in 20

Followed quickly by:

You may want to keep Pirelli away from your sock drawer. Reesie may have spilled the beans about your color-coding system for your ginch.

I roll my eyes. *Hockey players. We're ridiculous.*

When I finally open the door, Jamie's sprawled across his bed, scrolling on his phone. His t-shirt has ridden up, exposing a strip of skin above his waist-band. I do not notice this.

"Mission successful?" His eyes dance with amusement. "Have you come up with a solid plan for how to reorganize the ice machine for better efficiency?"

Heat creeps up my neck. "You're hilarious. Team dinner in twenty minutes."

"Plenty of time to color-code my socks then." He shoots me a cheeky grin.

I busy myself with puttering around, rearranging shit that doesn't need it while refusing to rise to his bait. "We're meeting in the lobby."

"I'll try not to be fashionably late." He stretches, and that damn t-shirt rides up higher. "Though you should probably give me a detailed schedule. Preferably laminated."

I roll my eyes again. *Seriously. Hockey players.* "I'll meet you downstairs." I grab my wallet, needing to escape. "Don't be late."

The Italian restaurant is walking-distance from the hotel. Thank god, because I need the air. Jamie falls into step beside me as we trail behind the others.

"So." His voice is pitched low, just for me. "Do you alphabetize your protein bars, too?"

"Only on game days," I deadpan before I can stop myself.

His startled laugh hits me squarely in the chest.

The restaurant is noisy, warm, and smells amazing. Charlie immediately starts giving us a lecture about proper pasta-to-sauce ratios while Louis chirps him about British food. I end up wedged between Austin and Jamie at our long table, hyperaware of how close Jamie's thigh is to mine.

"Wine list?" Jamie asks the server in perfect Italian because, *of course,* he speaks Italian. His accent makes something flutter in my stomach.

Through dinner, Jamie charms everyone, drawing out shy Olivier with questions about Québec and trading chirps with Louis about goalie superstitions.

I should be relieved that he's fitting in so well with the guys. Instead, I'm distracted by the way his mouth moves when he speaks, the way his fingers tap against his water glass, the way he keeps finding excuses to lean into my space to grab the salt or reach for bread.

"Earth to Rylan." Louis's voice next to my ear snaps me back. "You gonna finish that?"

I realize I've been pushing the same piece of chicken around my plate for ten minutes.

"Just tired," I mutter. But when I look up, Louis is giving me a strange look.

The walk back to the hotel seems both too short and too fast. Jamie's chatting away beside me about some British murder mystery Charlie recommended, but my mind's stuck on what happens next. We're going back to that room. Our room. Where I'll be trapped watching his bedtime routine. Earlier on the plane he wouldn't shut up about his fancy silk sleepwear, and now I can't stop my brain from wandering. Does he actually wear those bougie pajamas? Maybe he sleeps in just his boxers.

Or maybe... fuck, I need to stop this train of thought right-fucking-now before—

"You okay there, Cap?" Jamie's voice is closer than I expected. "You seem tense."

I am so fucking screwed.

CHAPTER 8

JAMIE

The light from my phone screen is too bright in the dark hotel room. It's after midnight, but sleep isn't coming. The unfamiliar bed isn't helping, but mostly, it's the hyperawareness of Rylan lying only a few feet away. I can tell from his breathing that he's not asleep either.

"Can't sleep before a game, either?" I finally ask, keeping my voice soft.

His sheets rustle. "Not usually," he admits after a pause.

"Let me guess—too busy reviewing plays in your head?"

"Something like that." Another pause. "What's your excuse?"

I roll onto my side. I can barely make out his shape in the darkness. "New team jitters, I guess. I really want to play well tomorrow."

"You don't need to worry." His voice is quieter now, almost gentle. "The way you've been playing in prac tice... the guys notice that kind of effort."

"Even Coté?"

Rylan sighs. "He'll come around. He's... protective."

"Of you?" The words slip out before I can stop them.

The silence stretches on for so long that I think he's not going to answer. Finally: "Of the team."

Through the gap in the curtains, the city lights cast faint patterns on the ceiling.

"What was it like?" I ask. "Winning the Cup?"

"Magic." The warmth in his voice makes my chest ache. "Everything just clicked, you know? The kind of season where even your mistakes turn into goals somehow."

"That overtime winner in Game 6 was legendary."

He's silent for a while, and I wonder if I've said the wrong thing. Then: "Sometimes..." He stops for a second. When he starts again, his voice is rougher. "Sometimes I wonder what my brother would have thought. He was the one with all the natural talent."

Something in my chest squeezes tight at the vulnerability in his voice. He's never mentioned his brother, and it's almost like Rylan's cracking open a door he usually keeps locked up tight. Everyone in hockey knows about Nick Collings, the golden boy who never got his shot at the NHL. His death made headlines even in Boston, where I was a kid dreaming of my own future in the league.

"Does it bother you to talk about him?" I ask softly.

The sheets rustle again as Rylan shifts in his bed. When he speaks, it's barely a whisper.

"No, it's not that. It's—I don't do it often. It's been almost twenty years, but sometimes it's like it just happened."

Something in his tone makes my chest ache. It's not only grief, it's something deeper. It's almost like he's spent so long not talking about his brother that the very act of forming the words is foreign.

"What was he like?"

"He was..." Rylan's voice catches slightly. "Everything came so easy to him. Hockey, school, friends. He was so much fun to be around, didn't matter what we were doing. He was going to be a legend. Some scouts used to joke that he was the 'second coming of Wayne Gretzky, ' but I don't think they were joking. He had this way of seeing plays develop before they happened—like he could read the future or something."

"I've seen some of his junior highlights," I continue carefully. "There was this goal he scored against Kingston? Fucking incredible."

"You've watched Nick's games?"

"Of course. Any hockey nerd worth their salt has studied those clips." I pause. "My coach in juniors used to make us watch them. He used to say that Nick Collings was the perfect example of how skill and hockey IQ could combine to create magic."

There's a soft sound from Rylan's bed, like he's sitting up. "He had this big scholarship to the University of Michigan. It was a big deal for a kid from our little town in the middle of nowhere, Canada. Everyone knew he was going straight to the NHL after. The only question was who would win the draft lottery so they could take him with the first overall pick."

The pain in his voice makes me want to reach out, to offer comfort, but I stay still, sensing he needs to get this out.

"He'd taken his girlfriend out for dinner. Sarah. They'd been together since their second year." His voice gets rougher. "Some asshole was driving the wrong way on the highway. Blood alcohol was three times the legal limit. They..." He stops and swallows hard. "They died on impact. Both of them."

My gut twists. "Fuck, Rylan...."

"The police showed up at our house around 2 AM. Every single detail is burned into my memory. When my dad flipped the outside light on, they had snow on the shoulders of their uniform jackets. One of the cops had been my peewee coach a couple of years earlier." He gives a bitter half-laugh. "We all got up because it was weird... the doorbell ringing in the middle of the night like that. When the cops came in, they made me go back to my room, but I stayed at the top of the stairs to listen. I couldn't make out the words, but..." he stops to draw in a shaky breath, and I have to grip the bedsheet to stop myself from going to him. "The sound my dad made... I'd never heard a sound like that come out of a human being..."

The silence stretches between us for a moment. It's so much. So heavy. Part of me wants to recoil, to pull back from the memories of so much pain. But

Rylan *lived* through it. Before I can say anything, he continues.

"My mom held us together," he says quietly. "She was the strong one through all of it. She was amazing. And then..." his voice cracks, and he clears his throat. "Just over a year after Nick... Things were never going to go back to normal, but we were starting to feel like maybe we'd survive, you know? But she passed away from an aneurysm. Out of the fucking blue... One minute she was there, and the next..." He shakes his head in the darkness.

"Jesus, Rylan. I'm... I'm so fucking sorry." I'd known about his brother, and I was dimly aware that his mom had passed at some point, but I never knew how it happened. He keeps talking like he hasn't heard me. Like maybe he needs to get the words out.

"After that, my dad... broke. He started drinking. At first, only at night, but then he started during the day too. He was never able to go back to his job at the mill after my mom..." He huffs. "So these days, I spend most of my time waiting for calls from the cops or the guy who owns the bar in town, telling me he needs to be picked up."

"God, Rylan. I'm so sorry. It must be so hard," I say gently. "Watching someone you love hurt themselves."

"I'm all he has left." His voice is tight with something that sounds like guilt. "I left him alone, in that town, with all those memories." He takes another shaky breath.

"We were supposed to play in the league together, you know? That was what Nick and I used to talk about when we were little. We wanted to play side by side and win the Cup together." He laughs bitterly.

"Hey." I sit up because he needs to hear this. Maybe no one has ever told him this before. "Your success doesn't dishonor Nick's memory. And you're allowed to have your own dreams, Ry."

"You know what's fucked up?" His voice is barely a whisper. "Sometimes I wonder if that's why I'm so..." He gestures vaguely in the semi-darkness. "Controlled. Rigid. It's like if I can keep control of everything, maybe I can stop anything else bad from happening." He huffs again. "Stupid, right?"

"That's not stupid or fucked up," I murmur. "It's human." I pause before adding, "And for what it's worth... I think Nick would be proud of you."

His breath catches. It's barely audible, but in the quiet darkness, it might as well be a shout. I have to resist the urge to cross the space between our beds and slide in beside him. I want to pull him close and wrap my arms around him and somehow protect him from all the pain inside him.

But I don't.

The silence that follows is heavy. When he finally speaks, his voice is rough. "I don't usually... I never talk about him. Not even with Lou."

"Thank you. For talking about him with me," I say.

There's a pause before he answers. "Thank you." The words are simple, but there's a warmth in his tone that makes my heart race. "We should sleep."

"Night, Rylan."

"Goodnight."

I stay awake a little longer, watching the city lights play across the ceiling, thinking about how much trust he just placed in me. It feels bigger than hockey. Bigger than being teammates or roommates.

Eventually, I drift off too, lulled by the sound of his steady breathing from the other bed.

CHAPTER 9

RYLAN

The same playlist I've used for more than ten years pulses through my headphones as I tape my stick with methodical precision. The ritual settles my nerves and brings focus to the chaos both in my mind and in the locker room.

Pirelli, on the other hand, isn't quite as precise. His tape job is quick, almost careless. He's bobbing his head to whatever's playing through his AirPods, occasionally singing along under his breath. His energy radiates outward, infectious enough that even Austin cracks a smile.

"Okay, boys, you know the plan," Coach Shaw announces, striding through the room. "Keep it simple. Remember what we worked on. This might be preseason, but it's important. Stick to our game."

I tie my skates, left first, then right, like always. Jamie's already suited up, his helmet dangling from one hand as he chats with Charlie.

"Five minutes," Coach calls out.

Jamie catches my eye as I stand. His smile is easy and confident. "Ready, Cap?"

I nod, keeping my expression neutral despite the way my stomach flips at his casual use of the nickname.

The familiar sounds fill the tunnel as we make our way out. Skates on rubber mats, stick taps, the low murmur of the crowd filtering through. Jamie falls into step beside me, and his presence is both unsettling and grounding at the same time.

Focus, Collings. I force my mind back to the game.

When the puck drops, I win the face-off cleanly, sliding it back to Austin. The familiar rush of adrenaline hits my bloodstream.

Jamie streaks up the right wing, his speed creating space. I cut through the neutral zone, and Austin's pass hits my tape perfectly.

Two quick strides. Jamie breaks behind their defense. My stick is like an extension of my body as I pass to him.

The puck settles on Jamie's stick like it belongs there. One lightning quick move and he buries it top shelf.

Fifteen seconds in.

Jamie's smile blazes as he crashes into me, our teammates piling on. His joy is contagious. For a moment, I'm fifteen again, celebrating with Nick after a perfect give-and-go, just like that one.

We build momentum off that first shift. Jamie anticipates my passes before I make them. I find him in spaces that shouldn't exist. It's effortless and instinctive. Like we've played together for years.

We connect again. This time I drive wide, drawing the defense. Jamie loops high, patient. I feel him without looking, just like I used to sense Nick. My backhand pass finds him easily.

Another goal. Another celebration.

The bench is buzzing. Even Austin's usual scowl softens when Jamie sets him up for a one-timer that makes it 3-0 before the first period is over.

"Holy shit, Cap," Charlie pants during a line change. "You and Pirelli are fucking magic together."

He's right. Jamie reads the game at my speed, and he sees the plays develop the way I do. The way Nick did.

For some reason, the memory of playing with my brother doesn't hurt like it usually does. Instead, it fuels something warm in my chest as Jamie and I connect for another scoring chance. Nick would have loved this—the pure joy of hockey played at its highest level.

For the first time in years, I'm not playing the system. I'm playing the game.

Unfortunately, the magic doesn't last. Their defense tightens up, collapsing around Jamie and me whenever we cross the blue line. What worked in the first period turns into turnovers and odd-man rushes the other way, and by the end of the second period, the San Diego Destroyers have tied it up at 3.

The third period starts with a mess. A bad line change leads to their go-ahead goal, and we're behind for the first time all night at 4-3.

Our frustration mounts with each missed opportunity. Pirelli and I are still connecting, but the finishing touch has disappeared. We're all trying to recapture that first-period magic instead of playing smart.

By halfway through the third, Coach has managed to settle us down a bit. Jamie creates chance after chance as we push hard for the tying goal.

With two minutes left, Coach Shaw pulls Louis for an extra attacker, so we're six-on-five.

But their goalie stands on his head, knocking away everything we throw at him, and the final buzzer sounds with the final score of 4-3, Destroyers.

It's like a punch to the gut. A preseason loss shouldn't hurt this much, but the disappointment on my teammates' faces cuts deep. We had this game, and we let it slip away.

Motherfucker.

JAMIE

The locker room reeks of defeat and frustration as we file in. My gear's soaked through with sweat, and the weight of our 4-3 loss hangs heavy. My first game with the Sasquatch, and we couldn't hold on to a three-goal lead.

Rylan's already at his stall, methodically unlacing his skates. His phone sits on the bench beside him, and he keeps glancing at it. His jaw tightens each time it buzzes, which it's doing a lot.

Riley appears in the doorway, a sympathetic grimace on her face. "Sorry guys, but the media's waiting." First loss of preseason, new players, new coach... They're probably circling like sharks.

Before Rylan can look up from his phone, which has just buzzed yet again, Lou jumps to his feet. "I got this one." His voice carries that same amiable tone he uses for everything. It's like he's volunteering to grab coffee instead of facing down a room full of reporters after a brutal loss.

Louis catches Rylan's eye for a second. Most people would miss it, but I'm watching. They have an entire conversation in that moment: Louis offers cover, and Rylan gives silent thanks.

Austin's moving too, his broad shoulders creating a wall between the media entrance and Rylan's stall. It's subtle but deliberate. He positions himself like he's organizing his gear, but the angle's perfect to block any ambitious reporter trying to sneak a photo or catch Rylan's attention.

"C'mon, rookie," Louis calls out to Tanner. "Time to learn the fun part of the job." He throws an arm around our backup goalie's shoulders, steering him toward the door with that infectious grin.

The defeated silence continues after Louis leads Tanner out. Charlie's the first to break it, tossing his sweaty jersey into the laundry bin with theatrical flair.

"Well, that was a bit shit. Who wants to cheer up with late-night poutine? I found this place that uses real Québec cheese curds."

A few weak chuckles ripple through the room. Charlie's got a gift for diffusing tension. Maybe it's because he's British. Everything sounds better with that accent.

Rylan's phone buzzes yet again. He snatches it up, shoulders tensing as he reads whatever's on the screen. The phone disappears into his pocket, but his hand stays there, gripping it like it might explode.

I want to ask if he's okay, but I don't want to push too hard. Besides, Austin's still hovering nearby, radiating protective energy like a guard dog.

Through the open door, Louis's voice carries from the media room, smooth and practiced: "Yeah, obviously not the result we wanted, but it's preseason. We have time to work out the kinks and build chemistry with the new guys. That's what these games are for."

Charlie tries again: "Seriously though, this poutine place. Open till 2 AM."

Rylan's phone buzzes again. This time he doesn't bother to check it, just closes his eyes for a moment, the muscle in his jaw working overtime. When he opens them, they meet mine briefly before darting away.

My fingers itch to grab his phone to see what's got him so wound up. But it's not my place.

Louis's voice floats in again: "Yeah, Pirelli and Collings showed some great chemistry. That's something we can build on."

The room gradually empties as the guys finish changing. Louis returns from media duty, giving Tanner an encouraging pat on the back before heading to his stall. Through it all, Rylan hasn't moved, still sitting on the bench in his base layers.

I take my time arranging my gear since the bus won't leave for another twenty minutes. Rylan's usually the first one packed and ready, but tonight he's barely started undressing.

When his phone buzzes again, something shifts in his expression. A crack in that perfect control. His fingers tremble slightly as he pulls it from his pocket, and this time what he reads makes him inhale sharply.

I take a step toward him, concern overriding my hesitation. But Louis catches my eye, giving the smallest shake of his head.

Austin materializes between us, all business, as he starts talking about tomorrow's travel schedule. His voice is carefully steady. It almost feels like he's trying to ground Rylan in the present moment.

Charlie appears at my elbow. "So, poutine?"

"Yeah, maybe," I say distractedly. I can't stop watching Rylan's reflection in the mirror across the room. His shoulders are hunched, and his movements have lost their usual precision as he finally starts removing his gear.

Louis brushes past me, bumping my shoulder hard enough to get my attention. When I look at him, he tilts his head toward the door. It's a clear message: give him space.

Right. Space. Even though every instinct screams at me to do the opposite. To push past Austin's wall of protection and find out what's wrong. To take care of him...

Charlie tugs at my arm. "Come on, Pirelli. Bus is waiting."

Chapter 10

RYLAN

The door clicks shut behind me as I follow Jamie into our room. Charlie was trying to convince everyone to go to some late-night poutine joint, but I'm not in the mood. My dad's been calling and texting me nonstop from the minute I stepped off the ice. The problem is, I know what's coming. Today would have been Nick's birthday. My father has never handled this day well. Nick's been gone eighteen years, and it never fucking gets easier for either of us. Dad seemed okay when I talked with him earlier today, but I knew the chances were slim that he'd be able to stay that way.

I take off my suit jacket and hang it in the closet, ready to go for tomorrow. Dress shirt, underwear, and socks go into my laundry bag. I double-check that my clothes for tomorrow are pressed and ready. Everything in its place.

Jamie moves around the room with his usual casual grace, humming a random medley of Taylor Swift songs under his breath. His tie lands on the desk chair. He kicks off his shoes near the window, one standing on its heel and the other flipped over.

The chaos of his existence should irritate me, but for some reason I don't understand, the way his energy fills the space in my normally empty hotel room is almost soothing.

My phone vibrates against the nightstand. Again.

My hands tremble as my fight-or-flight response kicks in. If I don't answer, he'll just keep calling and texting, so I should get it over with. My pulse pounds in my throat. I *really* don't want to pick it up, but there's no way to avoid this.

The thought of my dad alone in that house, probably sitting in his old armchair with a bottle of Jack Daniels sitting on the table right beside him, makes my chest tight.

My fucking phone keeps buzzing. It's like it knows I'll never be able to ignore it.

I suck in a breath and swipe to answer. "Hey, Dad."

"That was some fancy skating tonight." His words are slurred, confirming what I already knew. "Your new linemate's got some moves."

My jaw clenches, and I pace between the beds. Three steps one way, three steps back.

"Yeah, he's good." My voice comes out steady, even though I'm far from calm. Years of practice.

"Reminds me of Nicky." A glass clinks in the background. Ice cubes, maybe. Or a bottle against the rim. "The way he handles the puck. Natural talent, like your brother."

The comparison hits me in the chest. I'd thought the same thing, but hearing it from my dad is different.

"Wasn't good enough, though, was it?" His tone shifts, turning sharper. "Four unanswered goals. Nicky wouldn't a let that happen."

My free hand curls into a fist as the familiar burning shame rises in my throat.

"We'll do better next time." The words taste sour.

Jamie's stopped whatever he was doing in the bathroom, making it too quiet in here. I step over to the window, keeping my back to that side of the room.

"Better." Dad laughs bitterly. "You always say that. Always tryin'a be better. But you're not him, are you? Never will be."

"Dad, maybe we should—"

"He woulda made it." The ice cubes rattle again. "First overall draft pick for sure. Everyone said so. If he hadn't..." His voice cracks.

Fuck. My legs are weak. I press my forehead against the cool window glass, trying to settle myself. The city lights blur below.

"Yeah, he would have," I murmur, the same words I've said a thousand times. They never help.

"Woulda been easier if it'd been you."

The whispered words hit me like a slapshot to the chest. I've heard them before, or at least versions of them. I know in my heart he doesn't mean what he's saying. It's the booze and the eighteen years of relentless pain talking. I *know* that. But all the air leaves my lungs anyway, and my knees almost buckle.

"Dad—"

"I'm sorry." He's crying now. "I didn't mean that, son. I'm sorry. I'm so fucking sorry. I didn't mean it. Christ, I'm sorry, Rylan."

There's a soft rustle behind me, and Jamie's right there. Concerned. I squeeze my eyes shut, willing myself to keep breathing. To keep standing. To stay in control.

"It's okay." My voice sounds far away, like it's coming from outside me. "Get some sleep, Dad. I'll call you tomorrow."

"Rylan—"

I end the call before he can say anything else. The phone slips from my numb fingers onto the carpet.

I keep my forehead pressed to the window, hoping in vain that the cool, smooth surface will ground me, but it's no use. I can't even focus on the city lights anymore. My eyes are blurry with tears, and the glass is foggy from my ragged breaths.

A gentle touch lands on my shoulder. I flinch, my muscles tensing.

"Hey." Jamie's voice is soft. "What's going on? Are you okay?"

I need to calm down. Can't let anyone see me like this.

"Fine." The word comes out rough. I clear my throat, trying to pull myself together. "Just need a minute."

His hand stays on my shoulder, warm and steady, and I desperately want to lean into his touch. But I can't.

"Your dad..." Jamie hesitates. "He didn't mean it. Whatever he said."

A harsh laugh escapes me. "You don't know that."

"No," Jamie agrees quietly. "But grief makes people say awful things they don't mean."

His thumb moves in small circles against my shoulder blade, and that simple gesture breaks something loose in my chest. Suddenly, I can't catch my breath.

"It's been almost twenty years." My voice cracks. "It shouldn't still..."

"Hurt so much?" Jamie finishes when I trail off. "I don't think that grief follows a schedule."

His other hand comes up to rest between my shoulder blades, the warmth of his palm seeping into my skin through my shirt.

"You don't always have to be okay, you know," he murmurs.

The gentleness in his voice is what undoes me. A shudder runs through my body.

"I can't..." It comes out as a broken whisper.

He rests his forehead against the back of my neck, moving so his chest is pressed into my back. His big body is solid and warm and... safe.

And for the first time in longer than I can remember, I break.

The first sob catches me off guard as it rips through my chest. Jamie wraps his arms around me, turning me away from the window. I should resist. Should pull away. Should keep my distance.

But I let him guide my head to his shoulder while I clutch at his shirt, desperately seeking an anchor. Something to hang onto so I don't shatter into a million pieces. The fabric grows damp under my face as I let him hold me while violent sobs wrack my whole body.

He doesn't shush me or offer empty platitudes. He stands still, holding me, running slow circles on my back with one hand while the other cups the back of my neck. His touch is gentle but firm. It helps to ground me.

The scent of the shampoo from the locker room fills my lungs, mixing with the warmth of his skin as it surrounds me.

Should be mortified at falling apart like this in front of anyone, let alone a teammate. But there's something about Jamie Pirelli that makes it seem okay.

His fingers play with the short hair at the nape of my neck, and a different kind of shiver runs down my spine. My sobs gradually quiet, but I can't force myself to pull away.

"I've got you," Jamie murmurs against my temple. The words sink into my skin.

My hands are still fisted in his shirt. I need to let go and put myself back together. I need to put that calm, professional, reserved armor back on. It keeps me safe. Lets me function.

But for just this moment, I allow myself to be held. I let myself feel something other than the constant, crushing, relentless pressure to be exactly who everyone needs me to be.

Jamie's heartbeat is steady and strong against my cheek. The rhythm helps calm me, and the vice grip around my chest begins to loosen.

"Fuck. I'm sorry," I mumble into his shoulder, my voice rough. "I don't usually..."

"Don't apologize," he whispers, his hand tightening on the back of my neck.

I feel limp and drained, but somehow lighter, too. It's a cliché, but I feel like I've let go of something I've been carrying for a long time.

He traces small circles at the base of my skull with the pad of his thumb, and I have to suppress a shiver. The touch is innocent, meant to comfort, but my body responds against my will, the blood rushing south to my cock.

Fuck. I shouldn't do this.

But I can't make myself let go.

CHAPTER 11

JAMIE

Holding Rylan while he breaks down about his dad feels both right and dangerous at the same time. Right, because after months of watching him carry everyone else's burdens, he needs someone to help carry his. Dangerous, because having him this close makes me want things I shouldn't.

He fits perfectly against me, all long limbs and solid muscle. I try to focus on being supportive, on being what he needs at the moment, but it's almost impossible when having him pressed against me sends shivers down my spine.

When he nuzzles into the crook of my neck, I almost stop breathing. And then—*holy fuck*—he presses his lips against my skin, soft and hesitant, just below my ear.

"Rylan?" My voice is embarrassingly weak. "What are you...?"

Instead of answering, he drags his lips along my jaw. He fists his hands in my shirt and trembles. Or maybe it's me trembling. Jesus Christ, I must be dreaming. There's no way Rylan Collings—straight, controlled, perfect Captain Collings—is kissing my neck right now.

"Tell me to stop," he breathes against my skin. "Tell me I'm reading this wrong."

Every cell in my body screams at me to pull him closer. But this is Rylan. Team captain. The guy I've been desperately trying not to notice because he's so off-limits. The guy who just had an emotional breakdown. I need to be the responsible one here.

Instead, my hands slide up his back of their own accord, pulling him closer. "Don't you dare stop," I manage roughly. *Fuck being responsible, I guess.* "God, Ry, I thought I was imagining it. The way you look at me sometimes, how you..."

He cuts me off with a kiss that steals the breath from my lungs. It's messy and desperate and nothing like the controlled way he does *literally* everything else. I make an embarrassing sound because holy shit, This. Is. Happening. Rylan Collings is kissing me like he's drowning and I'm air.

When he responds to the first touch of my tongue with a quiet, needy sound, it takes every ounce of my self-control to not absolutely devour him. He tangles his fingers in my hair, the gentle sting sending sparks of electricity down my spine.

Breaking away to breathe is like torture, but I have to know this isn't just grief or confusion driving him. I rest my forehead against his, trying to slow my racing heart. "Please tell me this isn't just because you're upset about your dad," I whisper, hating how vulnerable I sound. "Because I've wanted this—wanted you—for so long, Ry. But I don't want to put pressure on you... I mean, are you..?"

"I want this. I want you. It's not the thing with my dad." His voice is rough in a way I've never heard before, and it *does things* to me. "I've been fighting this since the first time we met... Since we shook hands in Carson's office..."

I frame his face with my hands, stroking my thumbs over those ridiculous cheekbones I've been dying to touch for months. "Yeah?" I hate how hopeful I sound, but I can't help it. This is the guy I've been trying so hard not to think about. "Because I've been going crazy, trying not to want you. Trying to convince myself I was seeing things that weren't there, reading this shit all wrong."

"You weren't wrong." He leans into my touch like he's starving for it, and *fuck*, it does something to my chest.

"Jesus, Rylan, I had no idea..." All this time, he's been carrying this secret. *He's into men*. No wonder he's wound so goddamn tight. Hiding something that big is exhausting.

"That's generally the idea behind being in the closet..."

That startles a laugh out of me because his sarcasm is jarring.

"No one knows? Not even Lou?"

He shakes his head. "No one knows." He runs his hands over my chest, and the look on his face is like he's just discovered the secrets of the universe. "I don't want to talk about Lou."

But I need to be sure. I can't pressure him. "Rylan..." I brush my thumb across his bottom lip, fighting the urge to follow it with my tongue. "We don't have to—"

He cuts me off by surging forward, taking my mouth with an intensity that steals my breath. Gone is the hesitation from before—this kiss is pure need, and *holy fuck, I am here for it.* I slide my hands into his hair, angling his head to deepen the kiss, and the sound he makes shoots straight to my dick.

He tugs on my hair, just hard enough to drive me crazy. I want to touch him everywhere, want to learn every inch of him, but I force myself to go slow. Because this isn't just anyone—this is Rylan. The guy who folds his fucking practice jerseys, color-codes his sock drawer and probably arranges his protein bars by flavor.

But the way he's kissing me is anything but controlled. It's messy and desperate and perfect. When I slide my tongue against his, he makes this broken sound that makes me want to wreck him in the best possible way. To show him how good it feels to fully let go.

I trail kisses down his jaw, tasting salt and skin, and his pulse races under my lips. His breath hitches when I find a sensitive spot on his neck, and the sound goes straight through me. He holds onto my shoulders like he needs something to anchor him in a storm.

"Jamie..." His voice is rough and breathless, and the sounds he makes get more desperate as I place a line of slow, wet kisses along his collarbone. Hhis body arches into mine like he can't help himself, and it's so goddamn hot. I slide my hands under his shirt, and his tight abs jump under my touch as he lets out a whimper. An actual *whimper.*

"Can I...?" I tug at his shirt, needing to see him, to taste more of him.

He nods frantically, helping me pull it off, and *holy fuck.* I've seen him shirtless in the locker room plenty, but this is different. His chest is heaving, his skin flushed. The way he shivers when I run my palms over his pecs makes my mouth water.

"Please..." I don't think he knows what he's begging for, so I pull back to see his face. Something about the raw vulnerability in his eyes makes me pause.

"Are you okay?" I ask softly. He slides his gaze away, biting his bottom lip, but only for a moment. When he looks back at me, his expression is pure hunger.

"More than okay," he murmurs before taking my mouth in another searing kiss that makes me dizzy.

I drop to my knees, looking up at him as I press open-mouthed kisses down his chest. His eyes go wide, his pupils blown out with lust. His hands tremble as he cards his fingers through my hair.

When I mouth at him through his sweats, his whole body shudders. "Fuck, Jamie... I..."

"You can let go," I tell him, hooking my fingers in his waistband. "It'll be okay. Let me take care of you, baby."

I slide his pants down, and the sight of him fully naked, flushed and wanting, almost breaks my self-control. His cock is thick and perfect. He's already leaking, and I can't resist a taste. The first swipe of my tongue over his cockhead draws a broken sound from his throat that shoots straight to my balls.

When I wrap my lips around his tip, a burst of pre-come hits my tongue, salty-tangy and perfect. I take him deeper, savoring his weight as he fills my mouth. His thighs tremble when I swirl my tongue around the head again, and the sounds he makes are almost enough to make me come, untouched.

When I pull off to suck one of his balls into my mouth, his whole body shudders. When I look up, he's watching me with dark, desperate eyes, his bottom lip caught between his teeth.

I pull off, rising quickly and pulling his body against me before thrusting my tongue into his mouth like it's mine to claim.

"Bed," I growl. "Want to do this right. Need you against me."

I walk him backward toward the nearest bed while shedding my own clothes, barely breaking our kiss as we move.

When the backs of his knees hit the mattress, I push him down, following him onto the sheets.

RYLAN

I'm nothing but a ball of sensations—Jamie's heavy body pressing me into the mattress, his mouth hot and wet on my skin, the scratch of his stubble against mine. I should feel exposed and vulnerable, but instead, I'm electrified. Every touch is exactly what I've been craving my whole life but have always been too afraid to let myself have.

He works his way down my body with devastating thoroughness, learning every spot that makes me gasp and shudder. My hips buck against him, desperately seeking friction, but he stubbornly refuses to give me what I need. The wet slide of his tongue across my nipple sends jolts of pleasure straight to my cock. When he sucks hard, and bites down, a jolt of pleasure-pain shoots right to my balls, and I can't hold back a desperate moan.

"Fuck, Jamie..." My voice is wrecked, nothing like my usual controlled tone. But I can't help it—not when he's touching me like this. Not when it's like some of the missing pieces in my life are falling into place right before my eyes.

His curls are soft between my fingers as he moves lower, mapping my abs with his tongue. The sight of him hovering over my cock, looking up at me with those intense blue eyes... *Christ.*

When he finally takes me in his mouth again, the searing, wet heat is overwhelming. I fist my hands in the sheets, fighting for control, but then he does something with his tongue that short-circuits my brain. The suction, the heat, the perfect pressure—it's nothing like I imagined. It's about a million times better.

I'm teetering on the edge when he suddenly pulls off, moving up my body to capture my mouth in another searing kiss. Tasting myself on his tongue makes me groan.

"Want you against me," he rasps. "Need to see your face when you come."

The first slide of his cock against mine tears a desperate sound from my throat. He's so hot, so hard, and when he slides his hand between our bodies to line us up...*fuck*. His hand is big, but he can barely wrap it around both of us. We're both leaking steadily now, and he uses his thumb to spread our mingled precome down our lengths, making everything deliciously slick.

I can't stop watching where we're pressed together; the visual almost as overwhelming as the sensation. The contrast of his golden skin against my lighter tone, the way the heads of our cocks peek through his fist with each stroke, how his precome drips down to mix with mine... *Christ*. The sight brings me dangerously closer to the edge.

"Jamie," I gasp into his mouth as he tightens his grip. My hips jerk up involuntarily, dragging my cock against his in the slick channel of his fist. "Fuck, I'm gonna—"

"Yeah," he pants, twisting his wrist in a way that makes sparks shoot up my spine. "Come with me, Ry. Want to see you fall apart."

With his forehead pressed to mine, both breathing the same air, he drives us toward the edge. Every stroke sends jolts of pleasure through me, building and building until I can't hold back one more second. When I finally reach that peak, it's with his name on my lips, my whole body arching as my come splashes hot between us. His answering groan is swallowed by my kiss as he follows right after, our release mixing on my stomach as his hips stutter against mine.

Moments later, he collapses half on top of me, pressing soft kisses to my shoulder as we catch our breath. I should be planning damage control, should be panicking about what this means for the team, for my career, for everything. But my usually sharp mind is hazy with pleasure, and Jamie's warm weight against me feels too good to fight.

He reaches for something, his discarded t-shirt maybe, and gently cleans us up. The tender care in such a simple action makes my chest tight.

"You okay?" he murmurs, pulling me closer. A distant warning bell sounds somewhere in the back of my head, but I'm too wrung out to listen.

"Yeah," I manage, turning into his warmth. Deal with consequences tomorrow, I tell myself. Just... just for now, let myself have this.

He cards his fingers through my hair again, and I feel myself drifting. The last thing I feel is his lips pressing softly against my temple before sleep pulls me under.

CHAPTER 12

RYLAN

The first thing that registers is the warmth. Not just physical warmth, but bone-deep contentment. I let myself sink into the comfort, into the solid weight of the arm draped over me and the gentle breath ghosting across my neck. In this half-awake state, everything is right. I'm safe and warm in a little cocoon where nothing can touch me.

Then reality crashes in like a blindside hit.

Oh my god. Oh fuck. What have I done?

Every muscle in my body goes rigid as memories crash over me like a fucking tsunami. Jamie's hands on my skin. His mouth trailing fire down my chest. The way his whispered words made me feel wanted and cared for and safe. The way he looked at me like I'm something precious instead of something broken. The sounds he made when I—

No. Stop.

Nausea rises in my throat, bitter and sharp. My heart pounds against my ribs and cold sweat breaks out across my skin.

All my years of careful control, of keeping this part of myself locked away... all undone in one moment of weakness. Because Jamie fucking Pirelli offered me some comfort. Because he listened to me. Because he *saw* me, the real me, for the first time since my brother died. And like an idiot, I let my walls crack, let myself believe, just for a second, that I could hand someone else a piece of this weight I've been dragging around for almost half my life.

Behind me, he shifts closer, sleepily tightening his arm around my waist and pulling me back into his chest. He nuzzles into the back of my neck and drops a soft kiss on my shoulder, which makes me shiver with the force of my desire. *Fucking traitorous body.* All I want to do is melt back into him, to pretend for one more minute that this is something I can have.

"Mmm." His voice is gravelly and satisfied. "Good morning."

The way he says it is soft and intimate, like we're something real. Like last night was something more than a lapse in my control. It hits me like a body check, almost knocking the air out of me. This is worse than the biggest hit I've ever taken, because this pain is entirely my own fault.

Fuck. Fuck. Fuck.

I pull away from him abruptly, ignoring how cold I suddenly feel. Jamie makes a confused sound, propping himself up on one elbow. The sheet pools around his waist, and I force my eyes away from all that golden skin. From the marks I left there last night when I forgot myself.

"This was a mistake." The words burn like acid on my tongue. "A huge mistake."

Jamie sits up fully, all traces of sleep gone from his face, replaced by understanding. Like he expected this. Like he knew I'd break this thing between us before it could even start. "Hey, let's talk about this—"

"There's nothing to talk about." I start grabbing my clothes from the floor, my craving for order warring with my desperate need to escape. My hands are shaking so badly I almost drop the shirt I just picked up. "This cannot happen again. Ever."

"Rylan. Don't do this." His voice is so gentle it hurts. "Please don't shut down on me. Last night was—"

"*Stop*," I cut him off.

I *can't* talk about it. I can't talk about how I let myself believe, just for a moment, that I could have this. I can't let myself remember how good it felt when he touched me like I'm someone who's perfect and whole and desirable instead of the broken shell that I am. I can't let myself remember how right it felt to finally give in to this desire that's lived inside me for as long as I can remember.

"This was totally inappropriate! I'm—fuck! I'm, I've never—"

In an instant, he's out of bed, coming toward me, and, instinctively, I jump back. The hurt that flashes across his face makes me hate myself even more.

"This isn't who I am," I say, the lie bitter on my tongue. "No one can know about this. It was just—I was confused. I was upset after talking to my father. It was a... a moment of weakness."

"*A moment of weakness*?" His words drip with bitterness. "Is that what you call it when someone *sees* you? The real you? When you let yourself *feel* something instead of being completely in control every fucking second, like some kind of robot?"

"Stop." My voice cracks. "Please..."

"Why? Because I'm right?" He runs a hand through his sleep-mussed curls, his muscles tight with frustration. "Because you're scared of how right last night was?"

I don't answer, disappearing into the bathroom instead, clutching my clothes to my chest like armor.

I barely recognize the man in the mirror looking back at me—my lips still swollen and marks blooming across my neck and collarbone like a map of everywhere he touched me.

I trace a vivid mark above my collarbone with my fingertips, remembering exactly how it got there—Jamie's mouth hot against my skin, whispering sweet, filthy words while I gasped his name. I press into it, savoring the dull ache, before yanking my hand away like I touched a hot stove.

This is not who you are, I tell my reflection. *You don't get to be this guy.*

But the man in the mirror looks wrecked in ways that have nothing to do with the physical. My eyes are too bright, too vulnerable. I look... almost blissed out. Or, at least I did before I remembered who it is I'm supposed to be.

My hands shake as I put on my clothes. Fumbling and dropping the toothpaste, my hairbrush, my deodorant. I'm sure Jamie's wondering if I'm having some kind of seizure in here. Once my teeth are brushed and I've splashed cold water on my face, I take a deep, cleansing breath before opening the bathroom door.

When I emerge, he's pulled on sweats and a t-shirt. His walls are up now too, his normal, easy warmth replaced by cold distance.

"We need to be on the bus in an hour." My voice is steady, even if nothing else is.

"Right." His smile is sharp enough to cut. *"Captain."*

That word—my title, my responsibility—lands like a slap. But even though it stings, it's a helpful reminder. I don't get to just be whoever I want. I don't get to fuck around with teammates.

I grab the rest of my things, jamming everything into my bag haphazardly, telling myself I'll just have to deal with wrinkled clothes.

I need to leave. I have to put some distance between us before I do something stupid like turn around and kiss him. Like I did last night when he looked at me with those eyes and saw someone worthwhile...

Stop. Stop. Stop.

"I'm going for a run." I can't meet his eyes. "I'll shower in the hotel gym. I'll catch you on the bus."

I'm out the door before he can respond, running from the hurt in his eyes. From the memory of his hands on my skin. From how perfect it felt to fall asleep in his arms. From everything I can't allow myself to want.

But I can't outrun the voice in my head that sounds suspiciously like Nick.

When are you going to stop punishing yourself for being happy, little brother?

CHAPTER 13

JAMIE

The team plane gleams in the California sunshine as we cross the tarmac. The sharp scent of jet fuel mingles with fresh coffee, and the metal railing is cool to the touch as I climb the stairs to board.

Since I seem to be intent on torturing myself, I take the seat right across the aisle from Rylan's workstation. My stomach twists while he goes through his precise setup routine, but now I see the cracks in the calm, ordered front he puts on for the world. The slight tremor in his hands. The way his tie is a tiny bit crooked. Details I wouldn't have noticed before last night.

Sarah, our flight attendant, breaks through my mental spiral with her usual warmth. "Good morning, boys! Coffee's ready." She catches Rylan's eye and gives him a bright smile. "Black, two sugars for the captain?"

"Thanks, Sarah." His voice is steady and professional. As if he didn't fall apart in my arms six hours ago. Now, he's all crisp suit and perfect posture, every inch the respected team captain. Before last night, I would've been impressed, but now I want to mess him up again. To make him lose that rigid control like he did when he was writhing underneath me, begging for more.

The plane's recycled air feels thick as he arranges his workspace. Laptop aligned at perfect right angles to his iPad. Coffee positioned precisely to the right. Game notes spread out with military precision and those eleventy-thousand different highlighters at the ready. It's like he said last night: if he can control all the little things, maybe he can fool himself into thinking he can control the big things. Big things like whatever is going on between us.

Louis comes down the aisle and plops down into the seat beside mine. He glances between Rylan and me like he can sense the tension between us.

"Morning, boys. You two missed out on some great poutine last night. Gotta hand it to Reeses Pieces; drop him into any city, and the man can sniff out the best food in town."

Charlie's silly nickname earns a grin from both Rylan and me, and my stomach flips at the glimpse of his real smile breaking through this tension between us.

Rylan loosens his tie, and the mark I left below his collarbone flashes into my mind. It's not visible, but just knowing it's right there, behind the fabric of his dress shirt, is enough to send a rush of blood to my dick. Of course, I also know how his breath hitched when I put that mark there, how his fingers tightened in my hair, how his whole body trembled... Now, he won't even glance in my direction.

Jesus Christ, I need to get a grip.

The plane taxis, and I pretend to be absorbed in my phone while watching Rylan. He's going through Coach's game notes from last night, moving his highlighter across the page with mechanical precision, but he's been on the same paragraph for ten minutes. When we lift off, he grips the armrests so tightly his knuckles go white. I noticed it yesterday, but today it feels weirdly intimate. It's like one more secret I'm not supposed to know about him.

Louis stretches out beside me. "You good?" he asks, his voice pitched below the ambient noise.

I force my face into what I hope is casual indiffer-
ence. "Yeah, fine." *Lies.* "Just tired." *Well, that's true,
at least.*

"Uh-huh." Lou's looking at me like I'm a puzzle
he's trying to put together, but he can't quite make
the pieces fit. I yawn and give an exaggerated stretch.
"Stayed up late to review the game tape," I add. *More
lies. Actually, I was too busy watching your best friend
fall apart in my arms, but we're not gonna talk about
that.*

After the seatbelt sign dings off, most of the guys
settle in for naps, Lou included. Charlie's already
snoring softly, while the rookie, Gagnon, is absorbed
in some video game two rows up. Nobody's paying
attention to me and how I can't stop stealing glances
at our team captain.

He's still pretending to study his game notes, but
he's bouncing his leg. That's a new one. The Rylan
Collings I knew before last night was always still. Always in control. Now that I know what he looks like
when that famous control shatters, I can't unsee it. I
don't fucking *want* to unsee it. It was gorgeous.

The plane hits a patch of turbulence, and Rylan's
water bottle tips, spilling water all over his notes.

I pick it up from where it's rolled to my feet and grab some napkins from the seat pocket in front of me. I unbuckle and quickly scootch across the aisle into the seat beside him so I can help mop up the water that just drowned his neatly highlighted game notes. When I accidentally-on-purpose brush my hand against his, he jerks back like he's been burned. *Fucking ouch.*

Our eyes meet for the first time since this morning, and *Jesus*. The raw vulnerability in his gaze before he slams his walls back up nearly drops me to my knees. For a second, all the desire, fear, and shame that's warring inside him are right there, in those eyes. Fuck, I want to touch him. I want to pull him close and break down those walls the same way I did last night. I want to remind him how incredible it felt when he finally let himself go.

But I don't.

"I've got it," he says stiffly, pulling more napkins from his own seat pocket. Always so self-sufficient. So determined to handle everything alone.

Up front, Gagnon laughs at something on his screen. The sound is jarring inside our weird little tension bubble. Rylan dabs at his notes, and I pretend not to notice his shaking hands. The same way I have to pretend not to remember the way those hands felt as they explored every inch of my body last night.

I should get up and move back to my seat. Should put some distance between us. But I can't make myself move.

We hit another pocket of turbulence, harder this time, and Rylan shoots his hand out, grabbing onto my thigh, his eyes wide with fear. For one heartbeat, neither of us moves. His hand is warm through my dress pants, and his throat works as he swallows. His fingers flex against my leg and fuck, I may die right here on this plane, and it will have nothing to do with the turbulence.

But then he yanks his hand back again, knocking his soggy notes to the floor.

We both bend to retrieve them and fucking hell, he still smells so delicious. That mix of expensive cologne and something uniquely Rylan Collings that I can taste on the back of my tongue.

"I've got it," he snaps, but his hands are trembling so badly he keeps dropping the papers. "Please, don't." His voice is barely a whisper, but in those two words, his message is clear: *Don't make this harder. Don't remind me. Don't make me feel this.*

Lou makes a snuffling sound from where he's stretched out in his seat across the aisle, sleeping like a baby.

"Sorry about the bumps, everyone," the pilot says over the speaker. "We're going to change altitude to find some smoother air for you. Hope I didn't disturb anyone's nap."

After things smooth out, Sarah, the flight attendant, comes by to see if anyone's hungry for a late breakfast slash early lunch, but the thought of food turns my stomach. Rylan, however, isn't having the same issue, predictably ordering grilled chicken and steamed vegetables with no sauce. *The King of Control is back in the building, ladies and gentlemen.*

My problem is that now I know what happens when that control slips. I know the sounds he makes when he breaks down. I know the way his eyes crinkle at the corners when he gives one of those rare, genuine smiles. And I know how his perfect muscles all tense when he's coming apart.

But somehow, I'm supposed to sit here pretending I don't know any of those things.

Austin walks past, pausing to grab something from his bag in the overhead bin. His eyes narrow slightly as they move between Rylan and me. "Everything good here, Cap?"

"Fine." Rylan's voice is steady as he glances up at Austin. His captain's mask is firmly in place, not a crack showing. "Just reviewing last night's tape." He gestures to his iPad.

He chats with Austin easily, like nothing's different. As if what happened last night didn't shift the world on its axis. His voice is steady and professional—the same voice he uses for press conferences and team meetings. It's not the voice that whispered my name in the dark. Not the same voice that broke on a sob as he came apart in my arms.

Something in my chest cracks open when he laughs at something Austin says.

This is what it's going to be like.

Watching him carry on like everything's perfectly fine while I drown in everything unsaid between us.

How the fuck am I going to manage this?

CHAPTER 14

RYLAN

Two days of avoiding Jamie Pirelli, and I'm already exhausted. Not physically—that wouldn't be a big deal. This is a bone-deep weariness that comes from constantly monitoring every move I make, trying to keep my professional distance at the same time as my body screams to be closer to him.

The familiar roar of the crowd reverberates through the concrete walls of our locker room. Tonight is our first home game of the year, another pre-season matchup, this time against the Chicago Outlaws. The air crackles with anticipation. The arena is packed with Seattle hockey fans eager to check out this season's team. Under normal circumstances, the energy would fuel me, but right now it only adds to the pressure weighing heavy on my shoulders.

Jamie's in front of his stall, two down from mine, bobbing his head to whatever's playing through his AirPods. The curve of his neck, the way his curls brush his collar, the familiar rhythm of his pre-game routine. Every single thing about him makes my chest ache. I force my eyes away, focusing on taping my stick with mechanical precision.

"Okay, gentlemen," Coach Shaw says from his position near the door. "Keep it simple, stay with the plan, and build on what worked in San Diego."

What worked in San Diego. Right. *If he only knew.*

The first period is a blur of overthinking and disconnection. Every pass between Jamie and me is a split second off; our timing is completely shot. The crowd's energy fades as we struggle to find a rhythm. Even my connection with Austin is off. And the second line isn't faring any better.

"What the fuck is going on with you two?" Austin mutters during a TV timeout, shooting a suspicious glance between Jamie and me. "You're thinking too much."

He's right. We're playing like strangers instead of linemates who've been clicking in practice like we share one brain. The score remains tied at zero, but that's only because Louis is standing on his head in net, making saves that belong on highlight reels.

Halfway through the second period, though, something shifts. One of Chicago's defensemen, Morrison, who's built like a brick shit-house, crushes me into the boards. The impact knocks the air from my lungs, but even as I'm going down, I somehow know exactly where Jamie is. Pure instinct takes over, and I slide the puck through Morrison's legs in a perfect tape-to-tape pass.

When it hits Jamie's stick, it's like watching poetry in motion. He weaves through the Outlaws' defense and then dekes left before burying it, top shelf. The crowd explodes as he throws his arms up in victory.

Before thinking about it, we're crashing together in celebration, and goddammit, even through the layers of pads and gear, the solid warmth of his body against mine feels like coming home. Our eyes meet through our visors, and his are sparkling with joy. We're both high on the thrill coursing through us, and for just a moment, I forget why I'm supposed to be keeping my distance.

The goal breaks something loose, and we're back to playing on pure instinct, that magic connection humming between us like electricity. Jamie finds the back of the net twice more before the final buzzer goes: once off a no-look pass I thread through traffic, and again when I win a battle along the boards and find him waiting right where I knew he'd be. It's a natural hat trick. The ice disappears under a shower of caps as the fans go crazy.

"Now that's what I'm talking about!" Coach Shaw beams in the locker room after our 4-2 win. "That's the chemistry we've been seeing in practice. Amazing team effort, but I think we can all agree that tonight, Chuck belongs with none other than Jamie Pirelli!" He tosses our mascot, Chuck the stuffed sasquatch, over to Jamie.

Jamie's grin lights up his entire face as he catches Chuck and sets him on the top shelf of his stall. "Thanks, guys. Let's keep doing it just like that!" His eyes are sparkling with victory when they meet mine, and he shoots me a quick wink.

That wink hits me like a shoulder right to the solar plexus. The genuine joy in his smile is contagious, and as the guys surround him, offering more congratulations and rehashing the best moments of the game, the force of my desire nearly knocks me over. But it's more than just physical—so much more. Jamie Pirelli may be the only person in the world who sees right through my thick walls of bullshit and recognizes the person behind them. The person I stopped believing I could be a long time ago.

Then Charlie crashes into him with a triumphant shout, and the moment shatters. But the reality hits me square in the face: we're perfect together on the ice.

And that reality only twists the knife deeper when I remember all the reasons we can't let that perfection spill over into the rest of our lives.

CHAPTER 15

JAMIE

After the incredible game versus the Outlaws and the first hat trick of my pro career, the rest of the preseason flies by in a blur. We were able to close it out with a decent record. We weren't exactly dominating, but we played well enough to keep Coach Shaw's blood pressure in check. Unfortunately, last night's regular-season opener against the Vancouver Kodiaks was a different story. The chemistry between Rylan and me vanished without a trace. We couldn't connect on a pass to save our damn lives, and our timing was shot to hell. The ugly 3-1 loss has left a bitter taste in everyone's mouth, and even Charlie's offer to treat everyone to post-game poutine couldn't fix things.

Now, thanks to some sadistic scheduling genius, we're headed out for our first road trip since that night in San Diego. Six nights. Six fucking nights of sharing a room with Rylan, pretending I don't remember how he sounds when he comes apart under my hands.

My gut churns as I board the plane, spotting him already in his usual seat at one of the individual workstations. He's arranging his notes and tablet with that precise attention to detail I used to find amusing. Now it just reminds me of how carefully he's been maintaining his distance since our hookup. As if he can organize away whatever is happening between us.

Louis shuffles past, favoring his left side from last night's game. He catches my eye, giving me a look that makes me wonder exactly how much he's figured out. Before I can dwell on it, Austin materializes like a defensive wall, dropping into the seat beside Rylan. His eyes meet mine briefly, and he may as well be wearing a neon sign that reads: "Pirelli-free zone."

I retreat to one of the couches further back, trying not to feel like I've been banished. From this spot, I have a perfect view of my two linemates. I can see how Austin leans in every time Rylan speaks, and how his normally surly expression softens when Rylan looks away. And then it hits me like a kick in the gut: *Austin has feelings for him.* Suddenly Austin's hostility toward me and the way he seems to run interference whenever I get too close to Rylan all make sense. My stomach twists. *Shit*. Has he somehow picked up on what happened in San Diego? Or is he just being protective of Rylan in general?

Charlie flops onto the couch beside me, tablet in hand. "Ready for six days living out of a suitcase?"

"Yeah, should be fun," I manage, fighting to keep my voice casual. As if I haven't spent every night this week lying awake, alternating between dread and excitement at the thought of being trapped in a hotel room with Rylan again.

"First real road trip with the team." Charlie's tone is light, but his eyes are sharp. "Different vibe than Florida, eh?"

I tear my gaze away from where Austin's showing Rylan something on his phone, their heads bent close together. My stomach burns with jealousy, catching me off guard. "Oh, yeah. Very different," I answer with a forced smile that I only hope doesn't make me look deranged.

The plane takes off, and I pretend to review game film on my iPad while stealing glances at Rylan. His shoulders are so tense they must ache. Twice, I catch him beginning to turn and look back toward me, but he catches himself. The third time, our eyes meet for a fraction of a second before he whips his head back around so fast I worry he might strain something.

When Austin leans in and whispers something that brings that rare, genuine smile to Rylan's face, the one I've only seen a handful of times, I have to stop myself from getting up and... what? Marking my territory? What am I gonna do, pee in a circle around him like I'm a dog? *Jesus Christ, I'm losing it.*

This is going to be the longest fucking road trip of my life.

By the time we land in Minneapolis a few hours later, everyone's feeling the effects of last night's loss and the early flight. Although the comfortable reclining seats on the plane help, it's still going to make for a long day. We all shuffle through the hotel lobby, looking forward to getting to our rooms for a nap. In a couple of hours, we'll get together for a team lunch before the buses head out to the arena later on.

Rylan handles our check-in, passing me my keycard without so much as a glance, and then making a beeline for the elevators. I trail after him, trying not to feel like a lost puppy, and as I step into the elevator, I send out a silent plea to the Universe for us to make it directly to our destination with no unscheduled stops between floors.

While we don't end up getting stuck, the journey still seems agonizing. Rylan stands in the front corner, his posture stiff, while I lean against the back wall. The space between us may as well be the Grand Canyon. A man in a suit gets on at the fourth floor, and I swear he senses the tension in the air because he lets out a noticeable sigh of relief when we exit on our floor before he does.

Our room is similar to the one in San Diego: two beds separated by a nightstand, and floor-to-ceiling windows with a desk in one corner. Rylan claims the bed furthest from the door, setting his bag down with the same careful movements he uses for everything.

"I'll take the bathroom first if that's okay?" His tone is cool and professional, as if we're discussing line changes during practice.

"Yeah, sure." I try to match his tone, but my voice comes out rougher than intended. His shoulders tense, the only sign he's affected at all.

The moment the bathroom door closes, I collapse onto my bed, pressing the heels of my hands against my eyes. Charlie's earlier question echoes in my mind: "Different vibe than Florida, eh?" Yeah, no shit. In Florida, I was worried about getting hazed or bullied or finding slurs carved into my stall. Here, I'm trying not to jump my captain while pretending I don't notice how his t-shirt clings to his shoulders when he's stressed.

The sound of running water makes my mind drift to dangerous places.

This is going to be the longest road trip of my entire life.

The loss sits heavy in my muscles as we trudge back into the hotel after midnight. Charlie's trying to organize a group for drinks at the hotel bar, his voice carrying across the lobby. "Come on, just one drink. That game was brutal, mates. We need to decompress."

A few guys peel off to join him, but all I want to do is face plant into my mattress and forget this day ever happened. Rylan and I get into the elevator with Louis and Tanner, and even Lou's usually chipper outlook is subdued, making the silence in the confined space thick enough to choke on. A 7-1 loss will do that to a team. Now that silence has followed us into our room.

I'm debating whether I should force myself to be social, figuring maybe a drink will help blur the edges of this awkwardness between us, when Rylan's phone buzzes. He pulls it out of his pocket, frowning at the screen. It buzzes again immediately, and the color drains from his face.

A couple of minutes later, his phone vibrates again, and I can't pretend not to notice something's up. He's gone still, and it reminds me of the calm before a big storm hits. He's gripping his phone so hard his knuckles are white.

"Do you need me to call Louis?" I ask quietly, even though the last thing I want is to leave him when something's obviously wrong.

He shakes his head, still staring at the screen. Another buzz. His breath catches. It's such a small tell, but from someone so controlled all the time, it may as well be a scream.

"Rylan?" I take another step closer, unable to stop myself. "What can I—"

"It's Wally," he cuts me off, voice rough. "From the bar back home. My dad's..." He swallows hard. "He's on a bender. Talking about Nick."

The naked pain in his eyes when he finally looks up hits me like a body check. For the first time since that night in San Diego, there's no careful distance, no captain's mask. It's just Rylan, looking lost and broken.

"I don't..." he starts, then stops, his carefully constructed walls crumbling. "I can't..."

CHAPTER 16

RYLAN

My hands won't stop shaking as I read the latest in a long string of texts from Wally, the owner of the bar where Dad likes to drink.

> He's talking about Nick again.

> Trying to pick fights.

Fuck. The situation is heading downhill fast. The first text only came in while we were on the bus back to the hotel, less than an hour ago. If Dad's trying to start shit with other people already, it's going to be a rough night.

The familiar vice grip of panic tightens around my chest. Jamie's hovering close enough for me to smell his body wash, but he's not touching me. Always so respectful of my boundaries.

My phone vibrates twice more.

> *He just broke a tray of glasses. Not sure it was an accident.*

> *Had to take his keys. He's not happy.*

I close my eyes, drawing in a careful, controlled breath. *I can handle this.* It's what I do. What I've always done.

"Rylan?"

Jamie's voice is concerned. When I open my eyes, he's watching me with an intensity that makes my stomach drop. He knows too much—*because I told him too much*—about Nick, about Dad. *About me.* One night of weakness and I can't hide anymore.

"I need to make some calls." I grab my laptop bag. "I'll be in the business center."

"Rylan." His tone stops me at the door. "You don't have to do this by yourself. I can help you."

My throat tightens, and I almost turn back. Almost let myself indulge in the overwhelming sense of relief I felt that one night when I allowed myself to let go. When I let Jamie help me carry my heavy burdens for a little while.

My phone buzzes again.

I shake my head. "I—I gotta go."

The business center is mercifully empty. I choose the computer furthest from the door, my mechanical movements buying me time to think and plan and hopefully wrench back some control.

My phone buzzes. And buzzes. And buzzes.

> *Tried watering down his drinks but he noticed.*

I rest my forehead against the cool wood of the desk. *Think.*

I pull up my email, clicking through to my contact list. I used to call Lou's dad, Paul, when my father goes on a bender like this, but Paul and Jenny Tremblay moved to Palm Springs earlier this year. They wanted to be closer to their daughter, Lou's sister, Caley. Paul felt terrible when he told me they had decided to move, but Jesus, it's not like my dad's drinking should be their problem. They've saved my ass, and probably my dad's life, more times than I can count over the years.

I know I should have put some kind of emergency plan in place for this, but I stuck my fucking head in the sand. I wanted to believe Dad when he told me he was cutting back, so I let it go. And now that he's fallen off the wagon, I don't know who I'm going to call for help.

My fingers hover over the keyboard. Maybe I could try calling the bar; try to talk him down. But the thought of hearing his voice, slurred, angry, and full of grief makes my chest squeeze tight.

There's a soft knock at the door, and I know it's Jamie before I look up.

He's standing in the doorway of the business center, holding two cups of tea from the lobby coffee shop. His simple act of kindness hits me right in the gut.

"I heard you tell Louis that you've been drinking chamomile when you're stressed..." He trails off, setting one cup beside my keyboard. "I can go."

"Jamie." His name slips out before I can stop it. He pauses, those blue eyes searching my face. I should send him away so I can keep my distance. Keep our relationship strictly professional: neat and clean and controlled.

My phone lights up, and this time it's a call from Wally.

Jamie's expression shifts. "Want privacy?"

I should say yes. Instead, I reach out and grab his wrist, my fingers curling around his warm skin before I can stop myself.

He sits in the chair beside me, scooting it close enough that his shoulder presses against mine. "I'm here. Whatever you need."

I answer the phone on speaker, and for the first time tonight, my hands stop shaking.

"I'm so sorry, Rylan." Wally's gravelly voice is full of sorrow. "I tried to cut him off, but he started throwing things, and I had to call the cops. I had no choice."

"You did the right thing." My Captain's voice comes out steady. "Is Constable Mitchell there?"

"Yeah, hold on."

There's a rustling sound, then: "Hey, kid." Dave Mitchell's familiar drawl. He coached my peewee team a lifetime ago. He was also one of the officers who came to our door the night Nick died. "Your dad's safe. We've got him in the cruiser. Karen's bringing him some coffee."

Jamie's shoulder presses into mine.

"Does he need to go to the drunk tank?" I ask. It's the same dance we've been doing since Mom died.

Because everyone in town knows my dad, and he's not dangerous when he drinks, we can often avoid the overnight stay in the local RCMP detachment, but some nights there's no choice.

"Actually, Rylan... Your dad took a bit of a fall right before we got here. Knocked his head pretty good on the bar. I think he's fine, but I want to take him over to the clinic to get him checked out just to be on the safe side."

The room tilts slightly, and I close my eyes so I don't tip over and fall right out of the chair. Jamie's big arm wraps around my shoulders.

"How bad is it?" I ask.

"I don't think it's too serious. He seems pretty coherent. It's only a precaution, I promise. I'll give you a shout once we know what the doc wants to do, okay?"

"Um, yeah, okay." My voice sounds weird to my ears. It's like I'm hearing myself from underwater or something.

"Try not to worry too much, Rylan. I'll call you with an update as soon as I can, alright?"

"Okay, yes. Thank you." I say, and end the call before my control slips completely. Jamie's warm hand rubs gentle circles on my shoulder, and before I can stop myself, I'm leaning against him, allowing him to support some of my weight. Just for a minute.

"Come on," he says quietly. "Let's go back to the room."

"I should—"

"You can't do anything else until the cops call you back." His voice is soft but firm. "He's safe. He's going to be checked over by the doctor. Let's go back to the room."

I should argue. I need to pull away, thank him for his concern, and deal with this on my own. But I don't do any of that.

Instead, I let Jamie lead me to the elevator and back upstairs to our room with his hand warm against my lower back.

Just for tonight, I tell myself. After this, I'll go back to dealing with things on my own. Like I always do.

It feels like we're only in the room a few minutes, though I know it must be longer, when my cell rings, Constable Dave Mitchell's name flashing onto my screen. I don't want to think too hard about why I have the local RCMP officer's cell phone number programmed into my contacts.

"Hey, kid." Dave's voice is gentle in a way that makes my stomach clench.

"What did the doctor say?" I choke out, terrified.

"Your dad's going to be fine. Doc Matthews wants to keep him overnight for observation. It's just a precaution. They're going to patch up the cut over his eye and let him sleep it off. We got lucky tonight. They have an available bed."

Yeah. *Lucky.* Constable Mitchell doesn't say the other part: that my dad getting admitted to the hospital means he won't have to spend the night in the drunk tank. Again.

"Okay. Right." I say, closing my eyes and swallowing hard.

"But Rylan... this is the third time this month. Something's gonna give soon if—"

My chest tightens. "I know." I clear my throat before continuing. "Thanks for your help. I'm going to have to make some arrangements with my team, but I'll be home as soon as I can."

"Okay, Ry. You take care, kid." Dave's voice softens. "Your mom would be proud of you, you know."

"Thanks," I manage to choke out again. "I'll be there as soon as I can get a flight."

CHAPTER 17

JAMIE

Rylan's shoulders are rigid as he sets down the phone after talking to the police officer. He moves to his suitcase, probably looking for the comfort he gets from organizing stuff, but his hands are shaking so badly, he has trouble opening it.

"Here." I step closer, careful to telegraph my movements. "Let me help."

He lets out a shaky breath. "Jamie..."

"So, um, my mom is a psychology professor." I push forward. "She specializes in addiction treatment. She told me about this conference in Vancouver last year where she met a lot of people. I could... I could ask her for some advice if you want. She wouldn't have to know who I'm asking for, but maybe..."

Rylan goes still, and for a moment I think I've overstepped.

"Your mom." His voice is rough.

"Yeah." I give him a wry smile. "My whole family is full of brainiacs. My mom is an expert in her field, and she knows a lot of people." I move a little closer. "She has contacts all over North America."

He sinks onto his bed, holding his head in his hands. "I don't know what to do anymore."

"Will you let me ask her?" I pull out my phone. "I won't share your name. Nothing that could identify you."

His eyes meet mine, and the anguish on his face nearly takes my breath away. "Why are you doing this?" His voice is so broken it hurts my heart.

Because I can't stand seeing you in this much pain... Because you deserve to have someone help you with this heavy shit.

"Because you don't have to handle everything by yourself."

He gives a tiny nod. Taking that as permission, I text my mom while Rylan calls Coach Shaw. His Captain-voice is steady while he explains what's going on with his dad. Just like I knew he would, Coach Shaw tells him he should take emergency family leave. He tells Rylan not to worry about the team and reassures him he's doing the right thing by taking care of his family. I pretend not to notice how his free hand grips the bedspread while he talks.

My mom gets back to me almost immediately. She's still up, grading papers, and within a couple of minutes, she's sent a bunch of information about treatment centers, including the one in Vancouver she'd raved about after that conference. She also replied with an offer to do whatever she can to help speed up the intake process.

When I show Rylan her text, his eyes turn glassy and he swallows hard before whispering a barely audible "Thank you."

Carson calls next. His deep voice coming through Rylan's phone is concerned but supportive. From what I overhear, he says pretty much the same thing as Coach, assuring Rylan that this is why the league has an emergency policy and that he should focus on helping his father, not worry about the team. He ends by asking Rylan if he'd like Kelly to book his travel for him, but Rylan declines. When the call ends, he looks like a shell of himself: utterly drained.

"We need to book you a flight for tomorrow, right?" When he nods, I grab my iPad off the bed. "Okay, what airport do you fly into?"

Less than ten minutes later, I've booked him a flight to Toronto and reserved him a rental car. He doesn't say one word while I handle it, but I understand. He's going through enough. Doing this one small thing for him makes me feel less helpless—or at least not as much like a useless tit.

While he was talking with Carson, I changed into sweats and a comfy t-shirt, and throwing all caution to the wind, went into his things and pulled out a similar set of clothes for him. He still looks so fucking overwhelmed, I don't even ask permission, I just grab the clothes off the bed, take his hand and lead him into the bathroom.

I set his sweats on the counter before turning around and catching his eyes. "Do you want to take a hot shower?" I ask.

He shakes his head.

"Okay. Put your sweats on and hand me your clothes. I'll pack up while you brush your teeth, okay?" I keep my voice soft but firm. He hesitates, his blue eyes searching mine, but it's clear he doesn't have the strength to fight me. When he nods, I step out to give him privacy, and when he hands me his clothes, I fold them neatly and pack them in his bag.

When he comes out of the bathroom a few minutes later, I'm getting settled on my bed, my back resting against the headboard. "Come here," I say gently.

For a moment, he stands still. But then it's like something in him gives way, and he moves toward me, crawling onto my bed and lying beside me on his back, staring up at the ceiling.

"Yeah, no, that's not gonna work," I say, before sliding my arm underneath his shoulders and hauling him against me. He lets out a surprised huff but lets me manhandle him so he's pressed right up against me, our legs tangled together and his head resting against my chest. I wrap my arms around him and we lie quietly for a while, not speaking.

"Try to sleep," I murmur, running my fingers through his hair. "We'll figure everything out tomorrow."

He makes a soft sound, somewhere between protest and acceptance. But he doesn't pull away.

A few minutes later, he's still tense in my arms. So I start talking, keeping my voice low and steady.

"So, my whole family is full of ultra-brainy academics. Like, seriously brilliant people. My sister Lola is a constitutional lawyer in DC. She's argued cases before the Supreme Court. The woman is literally changing the world into a better place."

Rylan doesn't say anything, but he nods against my chest.

"My oldest brother, Adam, is a neurosurgeon. He lives in Boston, and he does groundbreaking research. He's a *literal* brain surgeon," I laugh. " And my other brother, Edward, works for NASA down in Houston. That brother is a *literal* rocket scientist. Then we have my parents..." I let out another soft laugh. "My dad is a department chair at Harvard, and my mom is a renowned professor of psychology, who also manages to keep seeing clients as her 'side project'."

Rylan shifts, snuggling in closer to me.

"And then there's me. The jock. The one who dropped out of Boston College to play hockey." My fingers continue their gentle path through his hair. "It's a whole 'one of these things is not like the other' scenario." I pause. "They support me, you know? I've never doubted that for one second. But sometimes I catch them exchanging these looks... Like they're waiting for me to wake up and realize I should be doing something more... important. More serious."

The tension has started draining out of Rylan's body, so I keep talking.

"I love them. And I know they love me, and I know they'll always support me. But I've always been the odd one out. The piece of the puzzle that doesn't quite fit." I take a breath. "I don't do anything to make the world a better place like they all do."

I swallow hard. "I don't think I've ever told anyone that before."

Rylan makes a soft sound, burrowing closer. His hand fists in my t-shirt, and something in my chest cracks wide open.

I hold him as his breathing evens out, keeping my own breathing steady and calm. Just before he drifts off, he mumbles something that might be "thank you."

"Sometimes being different isn't wrong," I whisper. "It's just... different."

Finally, he drifts into sleep, his breath warm and steady against my chest. I press my lips to his temple, gently, so I don't jostle him awake. "I've got you," I whisper, knowing he's already asleep.

Outside, Minneapolis traffic hums. Rylan's warm weight against me anchors me as I stare into the dark, wondering when exactly I started falling in love with this man.

CHAPTER 18

RYLAN

Warmth. Safety. The thump of a heartbeat under my ear. I'm cocooned in a scent that's becoming way too familiar: Jamie Pirelli. His chest rises and falls in a steady rhythm, radiating heat through his worn t-shirt.

For one perfect moment, I float in that space between sleeping and waking, where nothing exists except Jamie's arms around me and his fingers tangled in my hair.

Then reality crashes back.

Dad. Wally's texts. The police. Dad. And then Jamie taking charge while my brain struggled to process. Jamie holding me–*fuck*.

My entire body tenses. Jamie's breathing changes tempo, but he doesn't wake.

I should move. Should put myself back together and—

My phone buzzes on the nightstand. It's probably Constable Dave with an update about Dad.

My brain screams at me to run, but he tightens his arms around me without waking up, and I let myself stay. I can't force myself away from this feeling of being safe. Of being wrapped up in his solid, warm body.

Jamie stirs. "Time's it?" he mumbles into my hair.

Here's the point where I would normally run and hide. Like I did in San Diego.

But Dad's in the hospital. Jamie's mom has contacts at treatment centers. And Jamie...

Jamie shared pieces of himself last night. Things he's never told anyone else. He trusted me. I can at least *try* to trust him.

"Early," I manage. "But I should check on my dad."

He loosens his arms, giving me space to move without completely letting go. "Want me to order breakfast? Your flight's not until nine."

His simple offer of practical help makes a lump rise in my throat. "Yeah. Thanks."

I sit up slowly, and Jamie's hand slides to my lower back. It's warm and steady. It grounds me and helps me feel even more safe.

"I forwarded you those treatment center details from my mom," he says quietly. "If you still want them. And she offered to answer any questions you have. I put her contact info in the email."

I should say no. Should handle this alone. I should...

"Thank you," I whisper. For some reason, accepting his help feels like jumping off a cliff.

I check my messages while Jamie climbs out of bed. Two texts from Dave Mitchell: Dad's stable, got some decent sleep. Doc Matthews wants to run a couple more tests this morning.

I shake my head. Fuck, I'm lucky. Not many police officers would not only take the town drunk to the health clinic instead of tossing him into a jail cell to sober up but would also check up on the drunk in the morning, long after his shift has ended, and report back to the family. Like I said: real lucky.

Jamie moves around the room, somehow giving me the space I need while still being present with me. He's already ordered breakfast and pulled up my flight details. "Your Uber will be here in about forty-five minutes."

"Thanks." My voice comes out rough. I clear my throat. "I should pack."

"Already started." He gestures to my open suitcase with most of my clothes folded neatly inside. "Hope that's okay." He chews on his lip, looking uncertain.

It's more than okay. My jaw drops. "So you *can* be neat and organized!"

For a second, he looks as surprised as I am at the joke. *Who am I right now?* But then he shoots me a wink. "Eh, if the situation demands it, I can rise to almost *any* occasion." He waggles his eyebrows at me.

My phone buzzes again. It's Carson, confirming my leave. He insists I take at least three days.

"The team will understand," Jamie says after I end the call. He's arranging my toiletries. "We've got this for you. I promise."

"I should talk to Louis before—"

"I already texted him. He's meeting us for coffee downstairs before your ride gets here."

Us. Like we're a unit. I don't want to admit how good that feels. Having someone to help me. Someone to just be there. For me.

I should protest. I should keep my boundaries secure and remain professional. But I can't do it. The feeling of having someone look out for me is addictive.

A knock on the door announces breakfast. Jamie answers while I'm still frozen in place, struggling with how to handle all this... care.

"Eat first," he says, setting a plate in front of me. "Everything else can wait ten minutes."

"Jamie." His name comes out somewhere between grateful and panicked.

Our eyes lock, and that connection settles something inside me.

"I know this is hard for you—accepting help," he says. "But just... let me do this, okay? Please?" He's so sincere. He so genuinely wants to help me with my fucking mess of a life. I can barely comprehend it until I imagine the situation was reversed. And I realize I'd do anything in my power to make his life easier.

The lump in my throat threatens to choke me, but I manage to nod.

"Good." His smile is soft. "Now eat your eggs before they get cold. Louis will kill me if I let you leave with an empty stomach."

A laugh escapes before I can stop it. "You're ridiculous."

"Maybe." He shrugs, but his eyes are warm. "Is it working?"

More than you'll ever know... "Shut up and pass the coffee." I wink at him. *I fucking wink.*

I don't pull away when his hand brushes mine as he hands me the mug. Black coffee with two sugars.

Baby steps.

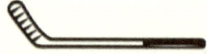

Louis is already in the lobby when we step off the elevator, three coffee cups on the table in front of him. His usual mischievous grin is nowhere in sight.

Jamie's knee presses against mine under the table, and I have to fight not to lean into his warmth. Not out in the open like this. The early morning lobby is mostly empty, but my skin prickles with paranoia anyway.

"My folks send their love," Lou continues, and my chest tightens at the mention of his parents. The Tremblays were my second family after Mom died.

Their kitchen table was a refuge I desperately needed when my dad started drinking. "Mom is furious
she's not there to help, but she's making calls. Apparently, she's still friends with half the nurses in
Northern Ontario."

"Thanks." I clear my throat. "For handling stuff
while I'm gone."

"Don't worry about the team." Lou's voice is
firm. "We've got this covered. You just focus on
your dad."

I nod, not trusting my voice. Jamie's hand finds
my knee under the table, squeezing gently before he
pulls away.

"And Ry?" Lou's expression softens. "Let people
help this time, yeah? No more lone wolf bullshit."

I want to protest so I can keep that careful distance that's always been between me and everyone
else. Including my best friend.

But Jamie's warm hand returns to my knee,
squeezing it again, reminding me that he's right
here beside me. That I'm going to be okay. And
Lou's watching me with thirty years of friendship
in his eyes. *Maybe...*

"Yeah," I manage. "Okay."

Lou's eyebrows shoot up, but he doesn't comment at the way I agree to accept help without argument.

Jamie stands, checking his phone. "Your Uber's three minutes out."

I get up too fast, almost sending my coffee flying. Jamie steadies it without a word, as if he was somehow expecting it to happen.

"Thanks," I say. *For the coffee save. For last night. For everything.* The word isn't nearly enough, but something in his eyes tells me he understands.

When he looks at me, Jamie's eyes are soft in a way I can't handle right now. I manage an awkward bro-hug, pulling back before I do something stupid like nuzzle my face into his neck and take a big lungful of his comforting scent.

"Text when you land?" he asks.

I nod, not trusting my voice. Lou pretends not to notice the... whatever it is that's going on between us.

"Come on," Lou grabs my bag. "I'll walk you down."

"So," he begins as we're walking across the lobby. "Pirelli was helpful last night?"

My heart rate spikes. Shit, has he noticed something? "Yeah," I swallow hard, my mouth tasting like sandpaper. "I'm—Yeah, he helped a lot, actually."

He turns to look at me as if he's seeing something he never has before. Dread crawls up my spine.

"I'm really glad," he says finally, his voice neutral in a way that isn't neutral at all. "It's good that you let someone help."

"Is it?" My laugh comes out bitter, and look down at my feet. "I'm supposed to be able to—"

"To what? Handle everything alone?" He cuts me off. "Like you've been doing since we were teenagers?"

"I don't—"

"Rylan." Something in his tone makes me stop. I lift my head to look at him, my heart pounding.

"Don't." His voice is gentle but firm. "I've known you too long, Ry. I see... stuff. Changes."

My heart pounds against my ribs. "Lou..."

"He's good for you," he continues, his voice soft. "Whatever it is... whatever label you want to use... I haven't seen you let anyone get this close to you since Nick."

I close my eyes, my heart racing. We're so close to naming it—this truth I've never been able to voice, even to my best friend.

"I don't know how to do this," I admit, my voice quiet.

"Do what? Accept help? Let people care about you?" He squeezes my shoulder. "You could start by not pushing away the people who want to be there for you. All of you."

The weight of what he isn't saying, the thing he's not forcing me to say out loud but seems to understand, makes a huge lump rise in my throat.

Something in my chest cracks open at the way he's giving me space to be honest without demanding I say something I'm not ready for.

"Louis, I—" The words stick in my throat. Years and years of hiding and suddenly I'm desperate to tell him everything. About Jamie. About who I am. About how fucking terrified I am to let anyone see this part of me.

"Hey." His smile is warm and genuine. The smile of a true best friend. "You don't have to say anything. Not until you're ready. I just need you to know that nothing changes for me. No matter what."

Tears burn behind my eyes. "How long have you...?"

"Known? Or suspected?" He shrugs, a small smile tugging at the corner of his mouth. "Remember juniors? That billet family's son who used to hang around practice?"

My breath catches. Michael. Dark-haired, quiet Michael who used to watch me when he thought I wasn't looking. Who I tried to never look back at. Or at least, not when anyone would notice.

"The way you avoided him," Louis continues carefully. "It wasn't because you didn't like him. It was because you did."

I have to grip the handle of my rolling suitcase to steady myself. All these years, and he knew. He *knew*.

"And now Jamie..." Louis's voice trails off.

"I can't—" My voice breaks. "The team, my dad, hockey..."

"None of that is worth destroying yourself over," Louis cuts me off gently. "Of course, I'd never say anything. But you deserve to be happy, Rylan. To be yourself. With whoever makes you feel safe enough."

The Uber pulls up to the curb.

Lou turns to me, his usual mischievous grin replaced with something fierce and protective. "Come here, you idiot."

He pulls me into a crushing hug, the kind we haven't shared since Mom's funeral. "I've got you," he whispers. "I always will. Nothing changes that."

My throat closes up. I grip the back of his jacket, struggling to swallow the tears burning behind my eyes.

"Thanks, Lou," I manage to choke out.

He pulls back, squeezing my shoulders. "Text me when you land. And Rylan?" His voice turns serious. "Stop punishing yourself for being happy. Nick would never have wanted that."

I can only nod, not trusting my voice. Lou grabs my bag, puts it in the trunk, and then watches the rideshare pull away.

My oldest friend. My fiercest defender.

I don't even want to allow myself to imagine what my life could be like if... *Fuck. Maybe...*

CHAPTER 19

JAMIE

I watch from the lobby windows as Louis gives Rylan a fierce, protective hug. It makes my chest ache.

Our awkward bro-hug was all Rylan could handle. That was all he was able to risk in public. I understand it, but that doesn't stop me from wanting more.

The Uber pulls away, and when he turns to walk back inside, his usually playful expression is deadly serious.

"So," he says, coming to stand beside me. "You and Rylan."

It's not a question. I keep my eyes on the street outside. "Is that... obvious?"

"To me? Yeah." His broad shoulders are tense as he pins me with his dark-eyed glare. "Look, Pirelli–"

"Jamie."

"Jamie." His voice softens a bit. "I've known Rylan Collings since we were kids. He's been through more shit than you or I can even imagine. And because of it, I've watched him build walls so high he can't see over them anymore."

I swallow hard. "I know."

"Do you? Because if this is just a hookup for you--"

"It's not." The words come out sharper than intended. I lower my voice. "It's not *just* anything."

Louis studies me for a long moment. "Okay," he says finally. "Good."

We stand in silence, watching morning traffic crawl past.

"At the meeting this morning," Louis says eventually. "Austin's gonna be suspicious as hell about why you helped him last night when he would usually call me."

Right. There will be questions. "What should I say?"

"Tell them you were awake when Rylan got the call from home, and like any good roommate, you pitched in to help in an emergency." He pauses. "And Jamie?"

"Yeah?"

"Be careful with him." His voice is gentle but firm. "He's... not good at letting people in."

"I noticed."

"But he's letting you." Louis gives me a look that holds over twenty years of friendship with Rylan. "Do not make him regret it."

The weight of what he's not saying, what he clearly knows about Rylan but isn't putting into words, sits heavy between us.

"I won't," I promise.

Louis nods once, and then his usual mischievous grin returns. "Come on, lover boy. Let's go face the inquisition."

"Fuck off," I mutter, but there's no heat in it.

My phone buzzes. It's Rylan:

> *Made it to the airport. Thanks for... everything.*

Three dots appear, disappear, and appear again. Then:

> *I'll call tonight*

Something warm unfurls in my chest. "Yeah," I whisper, too soft for Louis to hear, before I reply.

> You got this.

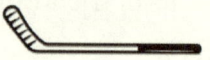

The pre-game meeting feels wrong without Rylan's precise routine setting the tone. No perfectly arranged notebook. No meticulously sharpened pencils. No...

Stop. Focus.

Austin's watching me from across the conference table as Coach Shaw reviews game footage. "Where's Collings?"

Coach Shaw had opened the meeting by announcing Rylan had to leave due to an unexpected family emergency and that he'd be back in a few days, but he didn't provide any details.

"It's his dad," Louis answers before I can, his voice pitched low so I'm the only one who can hear him besides Austin. "He'll be back in a few days. Ended up taking a fall and spent the night in hospital."

"Shit," Austin murmurs. "Was Roger...?"

"Yeah. He was." Lou answers Austin's unspoken question.

Lou and Austin are Rylan's closest friends, and they both know Ry's dad's situation, but I'm not sure if anyone else on the team does. I'm not going to be the one to tell people.

Charlie leans forward, concern clear on his face. "Everything okay?"

"Yeah, it's okay. Ry had to go take care of a few things for his dad up north. Just like Coach said." Lou smiles to take the edge off his words, but Charlie gets the message not to pry.

But nothing about this whole shit-tastic situation is okay. Rylan's dad being in the hospital, and the responsibility for all of his care falling on Rylan's shoulders alone isn't fair or okay at all.

"He's handling it," I say, proud of how steady my voice sounds.

Austin's still staring. "You were with him earlier this morning."

It's not exactly an accusation, but there's something dangerous in his tone.

Louis "accidentally" knocks over his water bottle. The loud clatter makes everyone jump and draws Coach's attention. "Sorry, sorry," he says with his usual grin. Then, quieter: "They're roommates, Coté. Cool it with the attack-dog shit, alright?"

I meet Austin's gaze. "He got the call from back home late last night. I was just trying to help where I could."

It's the truth, but the weight of what I *really* want to say sits heavy in my chest.

My phone buzzes with a text from Rylan.

> *Boarding soon. Try not to let* Coté murder my newest linemate while I'm gone.

Something warm blooms in my chest.

"Okay." Coach's voice cuts through my thoughts. "With Collings out for the next few days, we're moving Pirelli to Center, Reesie will be taking right wing and Coté will stay on left. We're keeping d-pairings the same: Santucci and Darbyshire will start."

Louis catches my eye across the table and mouths, "Breathe." It's like he can sense how much I'm struggling under the weight of all this.

I've got you, I'd told Rylan last night. Now I have to prove it by holding everything together here while he handles things with his dad.

I can do this. For him.

Coach drones on about neutral zone coverage, but all I can focus on is the empty chair beside me. Rylan's chair. Where he should be making those tiny precise notes in the margins, directing subtle looks at Louis whenever Coach says something particularly–

My phone vibrates. It's the airline confirming Rylan's check-in.

"Expecting something important?" Austin growls.

I lock my screen. "Family stuff."

"Pirelli." Coach's voice cuts through my thoughts. "You seeing something interesting in that power play footage?"

Shit. What are we supposed to be watching?

Louis jumps in smoothly, "I have a question about their power play cycling..."

I owe him. Again.

My phone buzzes. Rylan:

> *Made it through security. Thanks for packing my ID. I might have forgotten it.*

A smile tugs at my mouth. Because there's no way in hell Rylan Collings would have forgotten his ID. Not a chance.

"Focus up, boys." Coach clicks to the next slide.

Another text. Rylan:

> Try not to let Austin *overthink the C stuff tonight.*

Even while in crisis mode, he's still the team captain, working to lead us from afar.

"This morning's skate is optional," Coach continues. "But I want everyone's head in the game tonight. Minneapolis isn't going to go down easy just because we're missing our captain. Any questions?" He asks as finishes.

Several guys glance at the empty chair beside me, but no one asks for more details. They trust their captain, and they know if Rylan left on a game day, it must be important.

Trust I still need to earn.

"Alright, boys. Have some food, and get some rest. Check your schedules for bus times and meals. I'll see you all later."

As everyone files out, Louis catches my arm. "Coffee?"

"Can't." My phone buzzes again. "I need to—"

"Yeah." His smile is knowing. "Tell him we've got this covered."

I nod, my throat tight.

Austin pauses in the doorway, looking between Lou and me with narrowed eyes. But whatever he sees in my face must satisfy him, because he nods once before leaving.

My phone lights up.

Boarding now.

Three dots appear, disappear, and appear again. And then:

Thanks for having my back.

Of course. Anytime

"Yeah," I whisper, too soft for anyone to hear. "Always."

CHAPTER 20

RYLAN

I turn the rental car onto the street where I grew up, and my chest tightens as my childhood home comes into view. The white paint is peeling, and the garden is overgrown again, even though Dad promised he'd be better at keeping up with it. All this neglect started after Mom died, and she would be some pissed off if she saw the place now. She loved this little house.

I've offered countless times to buy Dad a new place, but he refuses to let me. This is where he raised his family, where Nick and I learned to skate in the backyard rink, where Mom tended her garden. "The only way I'm leaving this house is in a pine box," he always says.

Of course, my NHL salary could fix everything about this house except what's truly broken: the people inside it.

The key sticks in the lock like always, and as I step inside, I'm hit by the smell of stale beer with an underlying layer of musty neglect. It breaks my heart, but if I think too long about it, I'll break down before I lay eyes on my dad. So instead, I square my shoulders and walk down the hallway that's lined with old family pictures. Back from when we were an actual family.

The living room is dim despite the morning sun streaming in. Dad's in his ancient armchair, but he's not passed out, thank god. Constable Mitchell texted me about an hour ago to tell me he was released from the health clinic, and he got his wife, Karen, to bring Dad home and get him settled. I make a mental note to send them an incredible thank-you gift because, without their kindness, things would be a whole lot worse.

Dad's leaning back in his chair, his eyes closed, the white bandage above his eyebrow standing out in the low light.

"Dad?" My voice comes out steadier than I feel. "It's Rylan."

He opens his bloodshot eyes, and the shame in them catches me off guard. His expression isn't filled with anger and defiance like it usually is after an incident like this. It's just raw humiliation and naked pain.

"Hi,   son." His   expression   is   defeated. "You heard what happened." It's not a question, but I nod anyway.

"Yeah. Wally called me. And I talked to Dave Mitchell a couple of times. Sounds like it was a rough night." I move to open the curtains, but Dad raises a hand to stop me.

"Leave them." He swallows hard. "My head's killing me."

I raise an eyebrow. "Did they give you any painkillers at the clinic?"

He gives me a sad smile. "Just some Tylenol last night. But I deserve to feel like shit. I deserve to feel a lot fucking worse than I do."

Something's different about his tone. The usual bitter edge is missing, replaced by something more like resignation. Maybe it's the concussion, but this is new behavior from him. Normally, he'd be making excuses and playing the victim, blaming everyone else for whatever bad things happened while he was wasted.

I settle into my mom's old reading chair, and we're quiet for a long moment. "When I fell," he says finally. "Wally tried to help me, but I was pissed because he told me he'd called the cops. I..." His voice cracks. "I tried to fight him. Started swinging. At Wally Nelson, of all people. The only friend I've got left in this town after Paul and Jenny left..."

He touches the bandage gently, then shakes his head slowly.

"Doctor said I was lucky. Could've been a lot worse. Could've..." He trails off, but I hear the words he doesn't say. *Could've died.*

"Dad—"

"I saw your mother," he cuts me off, voice rough.

I blink at him. *Oh shit. Is he having delusions now?* "Um, what?"

He chuckles sadly at the expression on my face, and my stomach twists. "It's okay, Rylan, I'm not losing my mind. Yet." He sighs. "I know she wasn't really there. But when I hit my head, I swear to god, she was standing in front of me just as clear as day. And the look on her face..." He closes his eyes. "She was so goddamn disappointed in me." His hands shake slightly. "I get that it wasn't real, but..." he hesitates, taking a deep breath before continuing. "You know how people talk about loved ones visiting them in dreams?

Well, that's never happened to me. When your mom and Nick died, they were just gone for me. It didn't take very long before I couldn't remember what they looked like. I couldn't picture their faces or remember the sound of their voices. I had pictures, but I couldn't *see* them in my head anymore...if that makes sense."

I think about that. It's a little odd, but I guess I didn't experience it like he's describing. When I think about it now, I can still imagine my mom's smile, or hear the way Nick used to laugh when he teased me.

"Anyway, I just... It's been twenty years since we lost them, and the first time I'm able to actually "see" your mom, she's looking at me like she can't decide whether to break down in tears, or strangle me for being such a fool."

A snort of laughter escapes me because I remember that look of my mom's. When she looked at us like that, we knew shit was about to get real.

"Twenty years, Rylan. I've spent all these years trying to drink away the pain of losing them, and all I've done is waste the time I have left with the son I still have."

My throat tightens. "It's okay, Dad, you don't have to—"

"Yes, I do." He meets my eyes directly for the first time, and for the first time in as long as I can remember, he seems clear and focused. "I need help, son. Real help. Before I drink myself into the ground and leave you with nothing but ghosts."

Holy shit. Is this even real? I've wanted to hear these words from my father for so long, now that he's saying them, I can hardly believe they're real.

"That's... Wow, Dad, I'm happy to hear you say that." I don't know how to react. I'm scared of doing or saying something that will make him change his mind.

"So, I, um... I have a friend.... on the team. His mom is a psychologist, and she recommended a place," I say the words carefully, not wanting to break this fragile moment. "It's in Vancouver. They specialize in..." I trail off, unsure how to label his problems in a way that doesn't sound judgemental.

"Drunk old men who've wasted twenty years?" His laugh is bitter, but it doesn't have the angry edge I'm used to. "Who've pushed away the only family they have left?"

"Dad—"

"Your mother would be so ashamed of me." He runs a hand over his face, wincing at the movement. "And Nick... Christ, your brother would kick my ass if he could see me now."

My phone buzzes in my pocket. I ignore it, even though part of me wants to check. I already need the reminder that I'm part of another world, that I do have another life. One where not everything is so heartbreakingly sad.

"When can I go?" Dad asks quietly. "To this place in Vancouver?"

That catches me off guard. I'd spent the journey home psyching myself up for the usual dance we do around his drinking. The denial, the resistance to getting help. But this... I try not to let my surprise show. "I'll call and find out. If they can take you quickly, I'll go with you and make sure you're set up properly."

He nods slowly. "Good. That's... good." His hands twist together in his lap. "Will you..." He stops and swallows hard. "Will you visit? While I'm in there? I mean, I don't know how long I'll be... and with your schedule..."

The vulnerability in his voice makes my chest ache. "Of course, Dad. Vancouver's only three hours from Seattle. It'll be a lot easier to find time to visit."

"I haven't given you much reason to accept this," he continues. "But I'm so sorry, Rylan. You deserved a better father than what I've been."

I have to look away, as my eyes fill with tears. All these years of wanting him to acknowledge the pain he's caused, and now that he has, it's confusing me. I can't figure out how to react.

My phone buzzes again, and this time I pull it out of my pocket to check it, since I need a minute to collect myself. It's Jamie.

> "Charlie's threatening to reorganize your stall 'the British way.' Should I be worried?"

Despite everything, my lips twitch. The reminder of my life outside this sadness is so welcome.

"Someone important?" Dad asks. His tone of voice makes my heart race.

"Just a teammate," I say automatically. But then I remember Lou's reaction this morning. His easy acceptance.

Maybe... Maybe it's time to stop hiding.

The big knot of fear and dread lurches in my stomach, but I steel myself. I don't have to do everything at once, but maybe I can do a little. "Jamie Pirelli," I say quietly. "He's new this year. He's... been helping me with some stuff."

Dad's quiet for a moment, and I brace myself for... something. Judgment? Disappointment? But when he speaks, his voice is gentle.

"Good," he says simply. "You shouldn't have to handle everything alone."

The acceptance, however small, makes my throat tight. "Yeah," I manage. "I'm learning that."

The silence stretches between us, but it's different now. A little less heavy with unspoken accusations. It's like there's the possibility of... something. Healing, maybe. Or at least hope.

CHAPTER 21

JAMIE

When the puck drops for the game against the Minneapolis Stars, my body moves on autopilot. But everything seems off without Rylan.

The first period stays scoreless, but not for lack of chances. Austin and I sync up with Charlie pretty easily, leading to some great chances. But we can't execute. Our passes are perfect and our positioning is flawless, but there's no spark.

In the second period, Dallas scores twice in quick succession. We're able to claw one back on a beautiful play I set up for Charlie, but we're still in the hole.

As the clock ticks down in the third, we can't get anything going, and with two minutes left, they catch us on a bad line change, making it 3-1. In a mad scramble at the end, Coach pulls Lou and sends Gagnon out as the extra attacker, but it's no use. The horn sounds without another goal.

And now we've lost our first two games of the season.

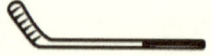

My hotel room is too quiet after the noise of the lobby bar. I lean back against the headboard, still in my dress shirt and slacks, unable to settle into my regular post-game routine. Everything feels off without Rylan's steady presence—the way he meticulously hangs up his suit, how he arranges his toiletries with military precision in the bathroom, his quiet strength that anchors me.

My phone buzzes. My heart speeds up when I see Rylan's name:

> "My dad asked to go to rehab. I'm taking him to that place in Vancouver."

> That's amazing news. How are you doing?

The three dots pop up and disappear a couple of times, and I can almost see him weighing each word, deciding how much to share.

> Okay. I think maybe we're both okay. For the first time in a while.

Somehow, his response feels less guarded than usual. Don't ask me how I can tell from a text. It's a gut feeling.

> Want to talk about it?

I hold my breath while waiting for his reply. *Say yes, say yes...*

Three dots again.

> Not sure I would know how. It's been a weird day.

I smile. Trust Rylan to call an emotional breakthrough with his alcoholic father 'weird.'

Before I can respond, he sends another message.

> I need to tell you something.

Well, fuck. My heart speeds up.

> What's that?

> I should have told you this sooner.
> In San Diego.

My hands start to shake. *Jesus, Pirelli, calm the fuck down.*

> You can tell me anything.

Those motherfucking three dots start, stop, and start again. My palms sweat as I wait for his reply. *Please don't end this. Not when we're just getting started.*

> You were my first.

It's like I've been cross-checked from behind. I read the words again. And then again. *He can't mean…*

> First what?

> First time with a man.

The words blur on the little screen.

> ~~Wait. What?~~

No, I can't send that. I delete it and try again.

> It was?

That's not much better, but I'm struggling with shock here.

Those goddamn dots taunt me. *Fuck it, I can't do this over text.*

My hands shake as I hit the call button. The screen is dark for a moment before he appears. His hair is messy, as if he's been running his hands through it—so different from his usual perfectly styled look. Hockey posters cover the wall behind him. He's in his childhood bedroom, and something about that makes my chest tight.

"Hey." His voice is soft, hesitant. He's shirtless, and even through the small screen, I can see the tension in his broad shoulders.

"Hey yourself." My voice comes out rough. The sight of his bare skin makes my mouth water, remembering how he tasted that night in San Diego. "So, um... That night was your first...?"

"Yeah—I mean—with a man. I've been with women... But... yeah."

All the air leaves my lungs in a whoosh. *Holy fuck. Holy fuck.* Memories from that night wash over me. How responsive he was, how he trembled when I touched him, how vulnerable he looked afterward...

"Rylan..." My heart is pounding so hard I can barely think. "Why didn't you tell me? I would have—"

"Would have what? Treated me like I was fragile? Like you felt sorry for me?"

There's a defensive edge to his words. *Shit.*

"No! Not—of course not. I just... I would have made sure it was special. Would have taken more time to..."

I trail off, remembering how desperate we were, how we crashed into each other. If I'd known it was his first time...

"It *was* special," his voice is more gentle. "It was amazing. Because... it was real. Because you saw what I needed. You saw me."

My throat closes up.

"Still," I whisper. "I wish you'd felt safe enough to tell me."

"I couldn't tell you then." He shakes his head. "Shit, I almost couldn't admit it to myself. But today, talking to my dad... Something clicked, I think. I just... I wanted you to know."

His raw honesty makes my chest ache. I want to tell him how much it means that he trusted me, but I'm terrified of pushing him too hard.

He swallows hard. "I... I'm not good at this," he manages.

"Not good at what?"

"At letting people get close to me. At being vulnerable." His eyes meet mine through the screen, dark with something that makes heat pool in my gut. "At wanting things."

"What do you want, Rylan?" My voice is gravelly.

The silence stretches so long that for a second I worry I've gone too far.

"You." It's a broken-sounding whisper. "I keep trying to stop, but... fuck, Jamie. I can't—I can't stop thinking about that night," he confesses, his voice cracking. "The way it felt when you touched me. You just—" he looks away, as if he's embarrassed. "It was like you knew what I needed."

"Fuck, Rylan." My cock throbs painfully against my zipper. "I just wish I'd known..."

"What would you have done differently?" There's that edge of challenge in his voice that drives me crazy, even as his eyes reveal his vulnerability.

"God, baby, I would have taken my time with you." I let my voice drop lower, rougher. "Would have laid you out and explored every inch of your body. Found all the spots that make you gasp and tremble."

His sharp inhale sends electricity down my spine. The rise and fall of his chest speeds up as his breathing quickens.

"Where would you start?" he whispers, and Christ, the way he looks at me through the screen—hungry and scared at the same time.

"I'd start with your neck." I trace my own throat, showing him. "Right here, where your pulse races. Then I'd move down to your collarbones... Fuck, Rylan, do you know how gorgeous you are? How perfect?"

He makes a strangled sound, his hand drifting down his abs. "Jamie..."

"Touch yourself for me," I breathe. "Please, baby. Let me see you."

He hesitates, that familiar need for control warring with desire on his face. "I've never... not like this..."

"I know. But you're safe with me. Always safe with me."

His tongue darts out to wet his lips, and fuck if that doesn't send even more heat straight to my cock.

"That's it, baby," I encourage when his hand slides lower. "God, look at you. So fucking gorgeous."

He makes a choked sound as he palms himself through his shorts. The fabric does nothing to hide how hard he is. "Jamie... I don't... what should I..."

"Take them off." My voice sounds wrecked already. "Let me see you. All of you."

His hands shake slightly as he pushes his shorts down, and Christ, the sight of him—flushed and hard and desperate—nearly makes me come in my pants like a teenager.

"Fuck," I groan, frantically working my own zipper. "Look what you do to me, Ry. How crazy you make me."

When I free my cock from my own pants, his eyes go dark and hungry. "Jamie..."

"Wrap your hand around your cock, baby. Jerk it nice and slow, just like I'd do it if I was there."

The sound he makes—half moan, half whimper—shoots straight through me.

"That's it. God, you're so perfect. Remember how it felt when I sucked you? When I swallowed you down and let you fuck my throat?"

"Fuck." His head falls back, exposing the long line of his throat. His hand speeds up. "Jamie, I can't—"

"Yes, you can. I've got you. Show me how good it feels. Let me hear you."

His usual rigid control shatters as desperate sounds spill from his throat while his hand moves even faster. I match my strokes to his rhythm, transfixed by the sight of him coming undone.

"That's it, baby. So fucking beautiful. Want to taste you so bad. Want to feel you come down my throat again."

"Jamie, please—" He's writhing now, his usual composure shattered.

"Come for me, Ry. Let me see you fall apart. You're so fucking perfect, baby, so—"

He comes with a broken cry of my name, his back arching off the bed. The sight of him completely lost to pleasure triggers my own release, and I follow him over the edge with a strangled groan.

RYLAN

I collapse back against my childhood bed, my chest heaving, Jamie's name still on my lips. Through the screen, I hear his ragged breathing slowly even out.

"Rylan..." The tenderness in his voice makes something in my chest crack open, and fear floods in, sharp and cold.

What have I done? This isn't—I can't—

"I should clean up," I manage, my voice rough. I need to rebuild my walls before they crumble completely.

"Hey." Jamie's voice is gentle. He knows me too well. "It's okay. We're okay."

I nod, not trusting myself to speak. The aftershocks of pleasure still ripple through me, warring with the rising panic.

"Get some sleep, Ry. Call me tomorrow?"

"Yeah." The lie tastes bitter. I know I won't. I Can't. This was too much, too raw, too—

"Goodnight, baby."

I end the call before his endearment can burrow deeper under my skin.

In the sudden silence of my childhood bedroom, I stare at the hockey posters on the walls—reminders of the straight, controlled captain I'm supposed to be.

Holy shit. What the fuck am I doing?

CHAPTER 22

RYLAN

The Vancouver rehab facility looks nothing like I expected. It's more like a fancy resort than a hospital. The buildings are all wood and stone in the Craftsman style, and they sit on a sprawling property overlooking the ocean in the suburb of West Vancouver, on the way up to Whistler. Walking paths wind through carefully maintained gardens, and the sound of waves crashing onto the rocks below reaches us as get out of the rental car.

Jamie's mom was able to make a call and get Dad into this place in less than 24 hours. Alexandra Pirelli has been added to my very long list of people who will be receiving extravagant thank-you gifts from me.

Thinking about Jamie sends a rush of heat through my belly as the memory of last night's video call flashes into my mind. But I push it aside. I need to be fully here for Dad right now.

We head toward the main building, Dad shuffling along beside me, looking smaller and older than normal. The tremor in his hands is worse than usual. I'm guessing it's nervousness, as well as whatever symptoms he's experiencing from not having had a drink today. After drinking for twenty years, I doubt his withdrawal is going to be like sleeping off a hangover. But this place has medical staff to help manage the physical effects so he can start working on the emotional stuff.

"Your mother would be proud of you, you know." His voice is gruff but steady. "Proud of both of us, maybe. Finally, facing our demons."

The words hit me hard. A couple of months ago, I wouldn't have believed Dad was capable of that kind of self-awareness. A few months ago, I was still pretending I could control everything in my life through sheer force of will. But that was before Jamie Pirelli crashed into my life and started knocking down all my carefully constructed walls.

"Let's get you checked in," I say, squeezing his shoulder as we walk through the automatic doors. The gesture feels foreign—we're not a touchy-feely family. But maybe that's something else that can change.

The admissions nurse greets us with practiced warmth and a genuine smile. She hands us a stack of forms, and Dad starts filling them out, his handwriting shaky but determined. He doesn't try to hide his tremors. He's not making excuses anymore. I hope that's a good sign.

The intake counselor leads us down a sunlit hallway to what will be his room for the next ninety days. It's simple but comfortable, with a single bed, a desk, and an ensuite bathroom. Dad sets his duffle bag down carefully, like he's afraid to disturb the quiet.

"You can help him unpack if you'd like," the counselor says. "Then we'll need to do some initial assessments." Her tone is kind but professional. No judgment, just facts. Jamie's mom sounded the same way when I talked with her about getting Dad in here.

We work in silence, folding his clothes and arranging his toiletries. The room slowly transforms from sterile to lived-in, although it still feels temporary. Like a kind of waystation between who Dad was and who he's trying to be.

"Ry." His voice catches as he pulls Nick's old junior team hoodie from his bag. The one Mom kept meaning to throw out when he first left for college, but never could. 'I've been wearing this lately. When things get... when I need...' He trails off.

My throat tightens. "That's a good idea. Keep it close to you," I manage. "Whatever you need to get through this."

He nods, carefully laying the hoodie on his pillow. "You should get back to your team." His eyes are clear and focused for the first time in a long time. And there's something new in them when he looks at me. It feels like understanding. Or acceptance. "Back to your friend, Jamie."

Heat floods my face, but I don't deny it. "Yeah. I should probably get going."

"Tell him..." Dad clears his throat. 'Tell him thanks. For his mother's help. For... everything."

"I'll visit," I say, surprised by how much I want to do it. "And when you're allowed, I'll call you. A lot."

Dad nods, his shoulders relaxing a little. "They said there's family therapy sessions... later on in the program. If you want..." He lets the invitation hang.

"Yeah." My voice comes out rough. "Yeah, that sounds like a good idea."

The intake counselor comes back in, her clipboard in one hand and a cup of coffee in the other. She hands it to Dad with an encouraging smile. "Ready for those assessments, Mr. Collings?"

He squares his shoulders. "As I'll ever be." He turns to me. "You don't need to stay for this part, son."

Something in his tone reminds me of Mom. That gentle firmness she'd get when she knew exactly what we needed. "You're sure?'

"I'm sure." He attempts a smile. It's rusty but real. "Besides, you've got a plane to catch. The team needs their captain."

I hesitate at the door, watching him settle into the chair across from the counselor. He looks smaller in the institutional lighting, but somehow stronger too. Like he's finally ready to face everything he's been drowning in whiskey for the past twenty years.

"I'm proud of you too, Dad," I say quietly. Then, before I can overthink it, I step forward and pull him into a hug. He stiffens for a moment. We haven't hugged each other like this since Mom's funeral, but when his arms come up around me, they're still strong, despite his shakes. We hold on to each other for a while, both of us pretending not to notice the other's damp eyes when we pull apart. And then I slip out before either of us can get more emotional.

Once I'm in my rental car, I pull out my phone. Three texts from Jamie, each one making my heart beat faster. One from Louis asking for updates. And a missed call from Coach, confirming our practice time tomorrow, while also telling me to take as much time as I need to make sure my dad is okay.

Real life waiting to resume.

But for the first time in forever, I'm not dreading it. Not hiding from it. Dad's doing the work to make himself a better person.

Maybe it's time I did too.

Chapter 23

JAMIE

The practice facility's parking lot is deserted when I pull in at 6 AM, Seattle's skyline barely visible through the pre-dawn fog. My hands shake as I punch in the door code. Two hours early for practice, because sleep was fucking impossible. Not with Rylan coming back today.

Every time I close my eyes, I hear those sounds he made during our call. That broken little gasp when he came.

Focus, Pirelli.

It's been a couple of nights since our video call, and I still don't know what it means. If it means anything. The texts we've exchanged have been carefully professional. They've been mostly about the team and a couple of updates about his dad. But nothing about us.

I need to get my shit together. I've worked too hard rebuilding my reputation here to risk it all going sideways. We only have one win in our first four games, and that's not good enough. I need to prove I'm an asset, not a liability. One more scandal with my name attached and all the trust I've earned disappears.

Greg, the early-morning custodian, waves through the glass as he resurfaces the ice. The familiar sound of the Zamboni should be soothing, but my heart's still racing. The locker room feels different. It's emptier without Rylan's precise routines setting our rhythm. His perfectly organized stall sits untouched, just the way he left it. Before everything changed.

"You're early, Pirelli."

My whole body goes hot, then cold. Rylan stands in the doorway, and fuck, he looks... different. Still hot as fuck in business casual instead of his usual suit, but there's something softer about his edges. It's like maybe some of that rigid control has eased a tiny bit. His eyes meet mine for a fraction of a second before darting away, but it's enough to send electricity shooting down my spine.

I want to push him against the wall and find out if his lips taste as good as I remember. Want to see if I can make him fall apart in person the way he did over the phone.

"Hey," he says, his voice neutral. But I notice the tiny tremble in his hands when he sets his bag down.

"Welcome back, Cap," Louis says easily, appearing from nowhere like the sneaky bastard he is. "How'd it go yesterday with your dad?"

"Better." Rylan's voice is quiet but steady. "Got him settled in Vancouver. The facility seems good."

I watch him move through his usual pre-practice routine, cataloging tiny differences. His movements are still precise but less... militant somehow. Like maybe he's not fighting himself quite so hard.

"Pirelli." My name in his mouth sends heat flooding through me. "You're here early."

I needed to see you. I can't stop thinking about you. I want to kiss you until you make those sounds again.

"Couldn't sleep," I manage, missing the casual tone I was aiming for by about a mile. My gear suddenly needs reorganization, giving me an excuse not to meet his eyes.

Charlie bursts in before Rylan can respond, his usual energy cranked to eleven. "Cap! You're back!" He practically bounces across the room for a fist bump. "I wanted to surprise you by reorganizing your stall, but they wouldn't let me."

Rylan's eyebrows shoot up. "You what?"

"Relax," Louis snorts. "We held him back. Your precious organization system is still intact."

Rylan's lips twitch, the ghost of a real smile, and my stomach flips. The urge to kiss that almost-smile hits me so hard I have to turn away. Fuck, I'm in trouble here. This isn't just attraction anymore. This is something else. Something terrifying.

The door opens again, and Austin appears, freezing mid-step when he sees Rylan. "You're back," he says softly, relief evident in his voice. Then his eyes narrow as he notices me. "You're here earlier than usual, Pirelli."

The protective edge in his voice sets my teeth on edge. I've seen how Austin looks at Rylan when he thinks no one's watching. Like Rylan hung the fucking moon.

"Didn't sleep well," I mutter, focusing on my stall. The last thing I need is Austin figuring out *why* I couldn't sleep.

"Seems like everyone's here bright and early this morning." Coach Shaw appears in the doorway, hands on his hips and an easy smile on his face.

"Just getting settled back in," Rylan says smoothly, but he shifts to put more space between us. *Ouch.*

"Can you pop into my office for a sec before you get on the ice?" Coach asks.

Rylan nods. "Yeah, of course." He follows Coach down the hall, and I can't stop myself from watching him go. His posture seems different... less tense than usual. Like maybe some of the weight he's been carrying has lifted.

"Earth to Pirelli," Louis's voice breaks into my thoughts. "You planning to actually gear up or keep standing there looking pretty?"

Heat crawls up my neck as I realize I've been standing with my practice jersey half-on, distracted by watching Rylan walk away. *Smooth, Pirelli.*

"I was, uh, admiring your, um, gear storage system," I stutter. "Very... organized."

"Unlike some people," Austin mutters, pointedly eyeing my more chaotic stall.

I paste a grin onto my face. "I try to embrace a philosophy of creative chaos."

"Children," Louis sighs and gives us an exaggerated eye-roll. "Behave, or Cap will put you both in time-out."

And holy fuck, the thought of Rylan forcibly putting me anywhere should not be hot, but imagining it sends a rush of blood straight to my dick.

***

By the time we hit the ice, I'm a hot mess. Being this close to him with all this... stuff... between us is killing me. And I can't stop thinking about the way he looked the other night. The sounds he made when...

Focus. Hockey. Think about hockey.

Coach Shaw blows the whistle, calling us in for drills. "First line, show me what you got."

Rylan takes his position at center, all business now. This, I'm ready for. This is hockey. Just like we've done a hundred times before.

Except it's not.

It's fucking electric.

Whatever's changed between us off the ice, our chemistry on it has only gotten stronger. Rylan anticipates my every move like he's reading my mind. Each play develops naturally. When I circle back behind the net, I know without looking that he'll be in position for the one-timer.

The puck hits his tape with perfect timing as he releases. Top shelf. Beautiful.

His eyes meet mine for a split second as the team celebrates. The intensity in his gaze knocks the breath right out of me.

"Looking good out there," Coach calls. "Run it again."

We're on fire. My body somehow knows where he is. Our passes connect almost effortlessly. It's goddamn poetry out here.

It's also torture.

"Bloody hell," Charlie mutters after our third perfect play. "Save some chemistry for the games, will you?"

If he only knew.

My body remembers exactly how perfect our chemistry was in San Diego. How incredible it was when his control finally cracked. How he felt under my hands. The sounds he made when...

Focus, dammit.

Austin's getting more aggressive with each drill, but never in Rylan's direction. His checks on me are getting harder, and his passes are a little too sharp when they're aimed my way. But with Rylan, he's still the solid, dependable linemate protecting his captain like always.

When he slams me into the boards during a rush drill, probably hoping I'll fuck up the play with Rylan, something in me snaps.

"Problem?" I growl, getting in his face before I can stop myself.

"Just making sure you're paying attention," Austin sneers, his eyes flicking toward Rylan.

"Hey!" Rylan's voice cuts through the tension. "What the hell, you guys? Cool it."

His captain's voice brooks no argument. But there's something else in his eyes when they meet mine. Something that sends a rush of blood south.

Jesus Christ, I need to focus.

"Line change!" Coach calls. "Second line up."

I skate to the bench, making sure to keep space between Rylan and me. But I can't stop watching him. The way he shifts seamlessly into Captain Mode, offering quiet advice to the rookies. How his hands move when he's explaining plays. Those same hands that gripped my shoulders in San Diego, that trembled when he allowed himself to touch me the way he wanted to.

The memory hits me so hard I almost miss Coach calling us back out.

This time, he has us running full-contact scrimmage drills. Which means I have to get up close and personal with Rylan. I have to battle him for pucks while pretending I don't remember what his skin feels like under my fingers. Or the way he gasped my name when I talked him through touching himself.

"Focus, Pirelli!" Coach barks as Rylan strips the puck from me for the third time. "Where's your head at?"

In a hotel room in San Diego. On FaceTime two nights ago. Everywhere except where it should be.

The rest of practice is sweet torture. Every time Rylan and I connect on a play, the electricity between us ratchets higher. And I know I'm not the only one affected. Rylan's breathing gets uneven when we're close, and he keeps unconsciously licking his lips, making me remember how they felt against mine that night.

Austin notices, too. His protective hovering gets more obvious as practice goes on, always finding ways to put himself between us. But even he can't deny our chemistry when Rylan and I execute a perfect give-and-go that leaves the defense spinning.

"Alright, that's enough for today," Coach finally calls. "Hit the showers."

Now I'm going to have to navigate the damn locker room without giving away how badly I want to push Rylan against his precisely organized stall and kiss him until he makes those sounds again.

CHAPTER 24

RYLAN

A couple of weeks later, the afternoon crowd at *Bean There Done That* coffee shop fills the air with laptop clicks. From our corner table, the tip of the Space Needle disappears into the low clouds. My phone sits face-up beside my Americano, waiting for the weekly update from Dad's rehab facility.

"So he's really doing the work?" Louis asks, stirring another sugar into his coffee. "Like, actually participating?"

"Yeah. The counselor says he's even volunteering to lead group sessions."

Austin shifts in his chair. "That's... good, right?"

"Yeah, it is." But this sense of hope is weird to me. I can't remember the last time I felt hopeful about my dad and his drinking. "They say the first thirty days are crucial. But he seems like he's genuinely committed."

"When can he have visitors?" Louis asks.

"After the first month." I take a sip of my coffee. "They want him focused on the program right now. No outside contact except for weekly email updates."

Louis's phone buzzes. "Charlie wants to know if we're coming for dinner tonight," he says, glancing at the screen. "Says he's found some authentic British pub that's 'proper brilliant, mate.'"

Last night, we closed out a six-game homestand, which means we've been in Seattle for over two weeks. We fly out tomorrow for our longest road trip of the season: an East Coast swing where we'll be playing six games in twelve days.

Our record is hovering around .500, and Jamie and I are racking up the points. Last night's goal was the latest example. I found him through an impossible gap in Calgary's defense with a pass that even I have to admit was a thing of beauty. Jamie responded by burying it top-shelf, in a goal that will make highlight reels.

Off the ice, things are... strange. After getting back to Seattle, I dove right back into my typical routine. I guess I'm a true creature of habit. We maintain careful distance, all professional courtesy, and measured interactions. But sometimes I catch him watching me with those blue eyes that see too much, and I remember how his voice sounded that night on the phone: firm and commanding, but still gentle as he told me exactly what he wanted me to do.

"Earth to Collings." Louis kicks me under the table. "You okay?"

"Yeah, sorry, just..." I gesture vaguely. "Got a lot on my mind." *That's the damn truth.*

"You going to do dinner?" Lou asks again, his voice softer.

"Nah." I shake my head. "Gonna pack and review some game tape. Lie low."

Austin straightens. "Want company?"

"Nah, it's okay," I swallow hard. "Gonna try to get a full night's sleep. Early morning flights are always a grind."

"Yeah, no shit. Gets harder every year." Lou rolls his eyes. I know he's been quietly rehabbing a strained groin for the last few weeks, but we haven't talked much about it. Tanner's been stepping up and doing a great job, but Lou's contract is up at the end of this season, so it won't be good if he's sidelined by an injury. He's going to have to play lights-out for the next few months if he wants a good offer from the team.

"Hey, Ry," Austin's voice pulls me out of my musing. "You know you can talk to us, right? About anything?"

There's something weird in his tone, and it makes my heart race. Shit, has he noticed the way I can barely keep my eyes off Jamie during practice? Has he figured out that I avoid being alone with him because I'm terrified I won't be able to keep my hands off him?

"Thanks, man, but I'm fine," I say, giving him a tight smile.

He gives me a look that says he's not buying it, but he doesn't push.

Louis's expression is knowing, but he nods. "I'll probably drop by the pub for a bit, but it'll be an early night. Text if you need anything?"

"Always."

As we walk out of the coffee shop together, Lou gives my shoulder a comforting squeeze. The gesture carries twenty years of friendship and unconditional acceptance. Sometimes, I wonder how he seems to know me almost better than I know myself.

Maybe I'm the only one who's still pretending.

***

My condo is way too quiet after the bustling coffee shop. Everything is right where it should be: throw pillows arranged at perfect angles, kitchen counters gleaming, Nick's old jersey hanging straight in its frame. But this afternoon, the familiar order that usually calms me only highlights the emptiness of the space.

I drop my keys in their designated spot, toeing off my shoes and setting them neatly on the rack by the door. Tomorrow night, Jamie and I will be sleeping in the same room. I've been trying not to obsess about it, but now that there's nothing to distract me, it's the only thing I can think about.

The video from last night's game loads on my laptop, but there's no way I can focus on it.

Fuck.

I slam the computer closed. Outside my window, Seattle's lights blur in the foggy, rainy darkness. A couple of hours north, in a Vancouver rehab facility, my dad's doing the hard work of facing his demons, and I'm sitting here like a coward, hiding from mine.

The weekly update from his counselor said Dad's been doing great. He's learning to talk about Mom and Nick without reaching for a bottle. It means he's finally beginning to process the grief of their deaths instead of numbing the pain with booze. Meanwhile, I'm still carefully arranging and micromanaging every aspect of my life, terrified to let anyone see who I really am.

Anyone except Jamie Pirelli. For some reason unknown to me, I cracked myself wide open and let him see inside. And then I bolted like a fucking coward. And after our FaceTime call, I got back to Seattle and pretended nothing had changed. I slipped right back into my usual habits of keeping everyone at arm's length, building my walls back up, brick by brick. But something's changed. I don't fucking want to be alone behind these walls anymore. But even if I wanted to knock these defenses down and let Jamie in permanently, I don't have the first fucking clue how.

A group text pops up. Pictures from the gathering at the pub. Jamie's in the background of one shot, laughing at something Charlie's saying. He looks relaxed and happy. Everything I'm not right now.

My phone buzzes again with a text from Lou.

> Sure you don't want to join? Charlie's teaching Olivier British drink-

> ing songs. Sounds amazing with
> his French Canadian accent.

I reply right away.

> Already in bed. Have a great time.

Lies. But there's no way I can face the guys right now.

A while later, I'm in my room, almost done packing, when my phone buzzes again with another text from Lou. It's close to midnight, so if he's still at the bar, it means he either found some girl to hook up with or he drank too many beers. Neither of those options will make for an easy morning. I grin as it buzzes several more times. Probably means he's had a few too many.

> hey Ry. you're my best friend any-
> one could ever ask for.

> Nothing will ever change that. No
> matter what. You can tell me any-
> thing.

> No matter what. I love you man.

I chuckle as I read the string of drunk texts from my best friend. I'm about to send back a snarky re-ply telling him to get his ass to bed, when the three

dots pop up and disappear a couple more times
He's probably having trouble controlling his
thumbs. The hazards of drunk texting. Finally, a
message appears.

> Ry I don't want you to hide any-
> more. You don't have to hide
> with me. I love you dude.

> Night Ry. Slp good

> Sory 4 drunk txts. Charlie brang
> me too many good beers :)

I reread the messages again and again. *What the
actual fuck? Does Lou know about me?*

Before I can spiral too far out of control, I close
my eyes and take a deep breath. I refuse to panic.
It's just Lou being Lou. He can get a little broody
when he drinks.

I finish packing and climb into bed, my mind a jum-
bled mess. Lou's right. Whether he suspects I'm gay
or whether he's just being goofy and I'm reading too
much into his drunk texts, he's still right: I *am* hiding. From my best friend, my family, my team... and
from myself. I've been doing it for so damn long, it's
become part of my personality. Hiding my truth from

everyone who loves me has become one of the central themes of my life. How fucking sad is that?

But the thought of everyone in the world knowing who I really am makes my gut churn. So I'm stuck. Caught between the guy I've always been and the person I could be, if I was fucking brave enough to try.

My perfectly organized apartment suddenly feels suffocating. All my careful routines and precise arrangements are nothing more than walls I've built to keep people out. And suddenly, it hits me: maybe these barricades I've hidden behind for all these years have kept out the danger, but they've also held in the pain.

My condo is still and quiet as I lie in my bed, alone. The carefully organized details of my life seem to be mocking me. My Dad's finding the courage to change. The team's finding its rhythm. Jamie's finding his place here in Seattle. And I'm still here, pretending I don't watch Jamie during practice. Pretending I don't remember every detail of that night in San Diego. And on that video call. Pretending I'm not falling for him.

Maybe Louis is right. Maybe I can't hide forever.

CHAPTER 25

JAMIE

"East Coast swing!" Charlie crows with his usual enthusiasm when I walk into the private terminal. "Ten days on the road, boys! Anyone up for cards? It's a long flight to Boston."

My stomach twists at the thought of playing in my hometown. Mom's already texting about dinner plans, and while I love my family, they can be a bit... much. I guess it will be nice to see them, but I'm preoccupied as fuck right now.

"Pirelli?" Charlie's voice breaks through my thoughts. "Cards?"

"Sure," I manage, risking a glance at Rylan. He's focused on the phone in his hand, but I catch the slight flush creeping up his neck.

It's been more than *two freaking weeks*. Two weeks of watching him rebuild his walls brick by careful brick. Two weeks of pretending that night on the phone didn't change a thing between us.

Oh, he's been perfectly professional. He's all "good work, Pirelli" while he keeps his distance, making sure we're never alone together. On the ice, we're still magic. Off the ice. Well, let's just say I could tell you exactly how many feet he keeps between us at all times.

And now we're going to be sharing hotel rooms for the next twelve days.

Fuck. Me. Sideways.

The hotel room door clicks shut behind us. After six hours of relentless turbulence, both atmospheric and emotional, everyone agreed to skip dinner and order room service. Even Charlie was too rattled to push for group bonding.

Rylan moves through the room with that precise efficiency I've gotten so familiar with, but there's something different about him. He's probably still rattled from the flight. Shit, even I'm rattled, and I'm not a nervous flier. But his usual perfect control seems... frayed.

"You can shower first," he says, not meeting my eyes as he unpacks his suitcase. His voice is strained, like he's working too hard to keep it steady.

"Rylan." His name comes out a little more harshly than intended. "We have to talk about this."

He freezes. "About what?"

"You know what." his shoulders tense as I step closer. "About how you've barely looked at me since that night on FaceTime."

"Jamie..." he whispers hoarsely. "I can't..."

"Can't what?" Another step. "Can't talk about it? Can't acknowledge that something is going on between us?"

He spins to face me and *fuck*. The look in his eyes nearly knocks me off my feet. "Of course, something's going on," he says, his voice cracking. "That's the whole fucking problem."

"Why?" I move closer. Close enough to see his pupils dilate. To feel how his breath catches. "Why is it such a problem?"

"Because..." He runs a shaking hand through his hair. "I can't control it. I can't control myself when you're near me. And I can't—" He cuts himself off.

"Maybe you don't have to fucking control everything." I take another step closer. "Maybe sometimes it's okay to just let shit happen."

"Like that night?" His voice drops lower, making heat pool in my gut. "When I let myself..."

"You were beautiful." The words are raw. "So fucking beautiful, Ry. Letting go for me. Letting me see you."

His breath hitches. "Jamie..."

"Tell me you haven't thought about it." I'm close enough to feel the heat from his body. "Tell me you haven't replayed every second of that night like I have."

"I can't." It comes out broken. "I can't stop thinking about it. About you. I'm losing my goddamn mind over it. I can't... I don't know what to do anymore!"

"It's okay." I reach toward him slowly, giving him time to pull away, but he doesn't. I brush my thumb across his jaw. "It is okay to let yourself want things, Rylan. It's okay to... to want me."

A shudder runs through his body, his eyes fluttering closed. "Jamie, please..."

"Please what?" I whisper. He trembles, pressing his head into my hand. "Tell me what you want, Rylan. Tell me what you need. It's safe. You're safe."

"I need—" He grips my shirt, curling his hands into fists. His eyes are closed, like he can't bear to look at me, but he doesn't push me away. He just holds onto me like he's afraid I'm going to disappear if he lets go. "I need you to make me stop thinking. Like you did that night. Like you always do."

"Yeah?" I thread my fingers into his short hair, and when he opens his eyes, his pupils are blown wide. "You want me to help you let go again? Want me to help you forget about everything except how good you feel?"

A broken sound escapes him. "Yes. Please."

The last of my control snaps at his broken plea. I surge forward, claiming his mouth in a kiss that's been building for weeks.

He opens for me immediately, and *holy fuck. He* tastes like coffee and mint and pure need. His hands fist tighter in my shirt as I back him up against the wall, slotting our bodies together like puzzle pieces finally finding their match.

"Jamie," he gasps when I move to his neck, finding that spot below his ear that makes him shake. "Oh god..."

"I've got you." I press closer, sliding my thigh between his legs. The sound he makes goes straight to my cock. "I promise I'll take care of you, baby. Let me make you feel good."

His hips roll against my thigh, seeking friction. "Please, I need..."

"What do you need?" I bite gently at his pulse point, feeling his heart race under my lips. "Tell me, Rylan. I want to give you everything."

"You." His voice breaks on the word. "Just you. So much."

I pull back to meet his eyes. He's so vulnerable right now. So terrified. But he's so goddamn beautiful. And the trust he's placing in me makes me feel like a goddamn king.

"I'm here." I brush my thumb across his kiss-swollen lips. "I've got you. Going to make it so perfect for you, baby. Going to help you let go of everything."

He surges forward to kiss me again, deeper this time. More desperate. It's like he's finally allowing himself to reach for what he wants. He slides his hands under my shirt, mapping my skin like he's trying to memorize every inch.

"Need to feel you," he mumbles against my lips. "Need all of it.."

"Yeah?" I work his buttons open, revealing more of his perfect skin. "Want me to take you apart, Ry?"

The sound he makes is half moan, half sob, and it nearly undoes me. I get his shirt open, running my hands over his chest, feeling his heart pound against my palm.

"Bed," I manage between kisses. "Need you spread out for me. I want to taste every inch of you."

He shudders hard, pupils blown so wide there's barely any color left. "Jamie..."

"I've got you." I walk him backward toward the bed. "Going to take such good care of you, baby."

CHAPTER 26

RYLAN

Jamie slides his big hands over my chest, leaving trails of fire across my skin, and something inside me finally breaks. All my careful control shatters under his touch. The backs of my knees hit the mattress, but I can't look away from the raw want in his eyes.

"Let me see you," he murmurs, fingers working my buttons open with careful reverence. "Want to memorize every inch of you."

He pushes the shirt off my shoulders, and Jesus Christ, the heat of his skin against mine is overwhelming. My breath catches as he traces each muscle with deliberate precision, like he's cataloging every detail. His mouth follows the path of his hands, dropping kisses along my collarbone, making my toes curl.

"Jamie," I gasp as he finds that sensitive spot below my ear. "Oh god..."

"That's it, baby." His voice is rough with desire. "Let me hear you. Want to know how good I make you feel."

My hands shake as I pull at his shirt, desperate to feel more of him. He helps me strip it off, and *fuck*—he's even more perfect than I remembered. All golden skin and defined muscle that makes my mouth water. The contrast between us is intoxicating, his sun-kissed warmth against my paler tone.

"Like what you see?" There's a hint of vulnerability in his cocky grin that makes my chest ache. Even now, after everything, he's still seeking reassurance.

"You're beautiful," I whisper, letting myself admit it. Letting myself want. The raw emotion that flashes across his face makes my heart race.

Then he's kissing me again, deeper, hungrier, pressing me back onto the bed. The weight of him above me feels like coming home. His thigh slides between mine, creating a delicious friction that has me arching up against him.

"Fuck, Rylan," he breathes against my neck. "The sounds you make..."

I should be embarrassed by the needy whimpers escaping me, but Jamie's hands are everywhere, setting my skin on fire, and I can't bring myself to give one tiny flying fuck.

His mouth blazes a path down my chest, his tongue flicking over my nipple in a way that makes me gasp. He slides a hand down, cupping me through my pants, and my hips buck up involuntarily.

"Please," I manage, not even sure what I'm asking for. *Everything. Anything.*

"I've got you." His voice is gentle but full of heat as he works at my belt. "Going to take such good care of you. It's gonna be so good."

My hands fist in his hair as he kisses down my stomach, his curls soft between my fingers. Each press of his lips feels like a brand, marking me as his. When he reaches the waistband of my pants, he glances up, his blue eyes dark with desire.

"Can I...?"

I nod frantically, unable to form words. He takes his time, slowly sliding my pants down my legs, his hands tracing every inch of newly exposed skin. The careful attention makes me tremble.

"So perfect," he murmurs, pressing kisses to my inner thighs. "Been dreaming about this."

I'm so impossibly hard I'm leaking. I'm practically dripping with need, but Jamie maintains his torturously slow pace. His tongue traces patterns on my hip bones while his hands stroke my thighs, and I'm practically vibrating.

"Jamie, please..." My voice breaks on his name. "I need..."

"What do you need, baby?" His breath ghosts over my cock, making me shiver. "Tell me."

"You," I manage. "Just... everything. Please."

The raw desperation in my voice seems to break something in him. He takes me into his mouth without warning, and the wet heat is almost too much. My back arches off the bed as pleasure shoots through me.

"Oh fuck, oh god..." The words spill out without my permission as he works me with his tongue. One of his hands slides up to pin my hip, holding me in place as he takes me deeper into his throat.

I'm a mess of desperate hands and needy whimpers as he brings me closer and closer to the edge. All my careful control has evaporated, leaving only raw need in its wake.

"Jamie, I'm gonna..." I try to warn him, tugging at his hair.

He hums around me, somehow taking me even deeper, and that's it. I'm coming harder than I ever have in my life, my whole body shaking as pleasure crashes through me in waves.

When I can focus again, Jamie's kissing his way back up my body, his expression soft but hungry. "You're so fucking gorgeous when you let go," he whispers against my skin.

I pull him up to kiss him properly, tasting myself on his tongue. His cock is hard against my hip, and I slide my hand between us to touch him.

"Show me," I whisper. "Show me what you like."

His breath catches as I stroke him. "Like that, just... *fuck,* a little tighter..."

I follow his instructions, cataloging his every gasp and moan, filing away what makes him shake. His face when he comes is the most beautiful thing I've ever seen.

Afterward, he gathers me close, pressing soft kisses to my temple. "You're amazing," he murmurs. "So perfect."

I turn my face into his neck, overwhelmed by the tenderness. For the first time in my life, I feel truly seen. Truly wanted. Truly... whole.

We lie tangled together, while he traces patterns on my skin with his fingertips, and I realize I don't want to put my walls back up. Not with him.

"Jamie," I whisper, meaning to say so much more. But he just pulls me closer, like he understands everything I can't put into words.

"I've got you," he breathes. "Always."

CHAPTER 27

RYLAN

The room is quiet, just our breathing and the faint hum of the hotel's air conditioning. Jamie's fingers trace lazy patterns on my skin, and I let myself sink into the sensation. Unfortunately, it's not long before reality starts creeping back in.

What are we doing?

"Hey." Jamie's voice is concerned. He must feel how I've tensed up. "I can hear you thinking from here."

I force myself to take a steady breath. I'm not going to panic and run like I did before, but I know we have to talk about... whatever this is.

"Jamie..." My voice comes out gravelly. "We should probably..."

"If you're about to tell me this was a mistake again, I'm going to strongly disagree," he says, his tone calm but firm.

I shift against him, needing to see his face. In the dim light, his eyes are serious despite his attempt at lightness.

"It's not a mistake. But it's also not... It's not that simple," I manage.

"Why not?" His hand stills on my shoulder. "Because you're not out? Because I am? Because we're teammates?"

"All of the above?" I try to pull away, but he holds me in place, and no part of me wants to fight him. "Jamie, I can't ask you to hide yourself because of me."

"You're not asking." His voice is firm but gentle. "I'm offering."

That stops me. "What?"

"Look." He props himself up on one elbow, his blue eyes intent on mine. "After Florida... I can't afford any drama. I can't have any more headlines about my personal life."

Understanding dawns slowly. "You... you want to keep this quiet, too?"

"For now." His thumb brushes my jaw. "Until we figure out what this is. Until we're both ready."

Hope flares in my chest. "Are you sure? Because it's not fair to ask you to hide, just because I'm too much of a cowar—"

"Hey." He cuts me off again, placing the pad of his thumb against my lips. "This isn't about you asking for anything. This is us making a choice that works right now. For both of us."

I search his face for any hint that he's just saying what I want to hear. But all I can find is sincerity and warmth.

"Jamie..." My voice catches. "It's not fair to you. I don't want to hurt you."

"I can decide what's fair to me," he says firmly. "And if you don't want to hurt me, don't run away again." His words are barely a whisper. "Let me have this much of you, at least."

The raw honesty in his voice undoes me. *Nick would've had the courage to be open about who he loved. He never let fear hold him back. But I'm not Nick, and Jamie Pirelli deserves better than a half-assed, secret, quasi-relationship.* Still, when I press my forehead to his, I know I can't walk away. "Okay," I breathe...

"Yeah?" His smile is hopeful. It kills me.

"Yeah." I let myself trace the curve of his lips. "But only if you're sure. I couldn't stand it if you grew to resent me."

"I'm sure." He catches my hand, pressing a kiss to my palm. "We'll figure it out together. Right now, let's just take it one day at a time."

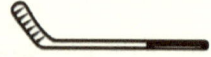

JAMIE

I keep my expression carefully hopeful as Rylan settles back against me, but my mind is racing. *What am I doing?* This is exactly the kind of complicated situation I promised myself I'd avoid after Florida. The last thing I need is more rumors, more speculation, more potential for scandal.

But watching Rylan's walls start to come up again, seeing that panic in his eyes... I couldn't let him run. Not again. Not after seeing how fucking perfect he is when he finally lets himself feel. When he leans into what he truly wants. Leans into who he is.

"You're sure about this?" he asks again, his voice small in a way that makes my chest ache.

"Absolutely." It's the truth. I'm sure I want it. What I don't tell him is how terrified I am of falling deeper into this. I don't tell him I can already feel myself caring too much, wanting too much. That I'm afraid I already want so much more than Rylan will ever be able to give.

His fingers trace patterns on my chest, and I try, unsuccessfully, not to shiver. "It's just... you've worked so hard to be open about who you are. To be a role model. And I'm asking you to go backward..."

"Hey." I tilt his chin up, needing him to believe this. "You're not asking anything. This is my choice too. And after everything in Florida..." I swallow hard, remembering the nasty headlines and whispers. "Privacy sounds pretty good right now."

It's not a total lie. The thought of more media scrutiny turns my stomach. But the bigger truth, that I'm already half in love with him and willing to accept whatever he can give me, feels way too dangerous to say out loud.

"There's no pressure, okay? No expectations. Just this. Just us."

Some of the tension leaves his body and guilt twists in my gut. Because there are expectations, aren't there? Every time he gives me a glimpse of who he really is behind all of his armor, it makes me hope for more. Leads me to imagine a future where we don't have to hide, where I can hold his hand in public, where...

Stop it. That's not what this is.

"We should get some sleep," he murmurs, fitting himself closer to me. "Early practice tomorrow."

"Yeah." I wrap my arm around him, loving how perfectly his body fits with mine. How right this feels, even though I know it's probably going to break my heart.

Because the truth is, I'll take whatever pieces of himself he's willing to share. Even if it means hiding. Even if it means watching him maintain his careful distance in public. Even if it means lying to myself about secret hotel room hookups being enough.

But then Rylan makes this soft sound as he drifts off. He's so trusting and vulnerable like this, in a way he never is anywhere else, and I know it's too late. I'm already so far gone for this man I'll take whatever he'll give me, and love it.

I press another kiss to his temple, breathing in the comfortable scent of his shampoo. I close my eyes and try to convince myself this won't end with my heart in pieces.

One day at a time, I think, echoing my earlier words to him. *Just take it one day at a time.*

Even if every day I fall a little harder for this man who may never be ready to catch me.

CHAPTER 28

JAMIE

The Boston Bears' rink smells like coffee and fresh ice at ass o'clock in the morning. I'm way too tired after being up half the night, but I still can't stop smiling as I gear up. That is, until I catch Louis watching me with raised eyebrows.

Act normal. Just act normal.

But normal feels impossible when Rylan walks in, looking unfairly composed for someone who's working on about three hours of sleep. Images from last night flash through my mind: the way his hands gripped my hips, his mouth hot against my neck...

Fuck. Focus.

"Morning, Pirelli," Charlie calls out cheerfully. "Ready for your hometown crowd tonight?"

"Fuckin' right, I am. " I shoot him a grin, trying to ignore my urge to walk over and claim our team captain right here in front of everyone.

"Just a light skate today, boys," Coach Shaw calls as he walks into the room. "Just enough to shake off the travel legs. Thirty minutes, then video review."

On the ice, everything should be easier. Hockey I can do. Hockey is safe, familiar territory where Rylan and I just... work. But somehow, knowing what he sounds like when he comes apart makes even our usual drills feel charged with new meaning.

"Nice feed," he says after I hit him with a perfect pass, his voice captain-professional. But there's a roughness to it that makes heat pool in my gut.

The puck hits my skate because I'm not paying attention. *Fuck.* Too busy remembering how Rylan's muscles felt under my fingers, how he gasped my name when—

"Focus, Pirelli!" Austin barks from the blue line.

"Sorry," I mutter, retrieving the puck. When I look up, Louis is watching me with an expression that's half amused, half concerned.

"You feeling okay?" he asks quietly as we circle back for another drill. "Seem a little... distracted."

"I'm fine."

"Right." Louis's tone is dry. "Just remember, there are a lot of eyes on this team."

My heart nearly stops. *Has he heard something? Did I do something already to put this thing in danger?*

"I'm careful," I say without thinking, then wince. *Way to be subtle, Pirelli.*

"Good." Louis taps my shin with his stick. "Some things are worth protecting."

After practice, I take my time getting changed and showered. I need to keep my head about me. Just because I have the urge to run around singing like some kind of Disney princess about how the colors seem brighter and the world seems like a better, more wonderful place today, doesn't mean I can actually do it.

"Anyone for breakfast?" Charlie suggests brightly. "That diner down the street had decent reviews."

"Can't," Rylan says smoothly. "Need to review some video."

"Same," I add quickly. Too quickly, based on the dirty look Austin sends my way.

"Right." Louis's voice carries a hint of amusement. "Well, don't work too hard."

As guys file out, I catch Rylan's eyes, and the heat in them goes right to my dick. I have to cover the way I suck in a sharp breath with a cough as I remember his promise that we would we'd "review video" together before the game.

God, this secret is going to kill me.

But fuck, watching him calmly go about his usual post-practice routine while we share this delicious secret... feels like it's worth it. Like he's worth it.

Even if I'm already terrible at hiding how much I want him.

***

Later that night, after our decisive win against the Bears, my family settles around the table at my mom's favorite restaurant. My dad and my brother Adam are already deeply absorbed in discussing some obscure literary theory. Adam the neurosurgeon, is somehow trying to connect it to his latest research. Don't even ask me how that's possible, I stopped trying a long time ago. Only my family could turn a hockey victory dinner into an academic debate.

"So explain again," Lola says, leaning forward with that lawyer's intensity she never quite turns off. "Why wasn't that last goal actually offside?"

I hide my smile behind my water glass. My constitutional lawyer sister trying to understand NHL rules is peak Pirelli family dynamics.

I start to explain, but Mom cuts me off.

"Never mind the technical details, darling. Tell me about your team. Are they being supportive? That team captain seems very..." She pauses, choosing her words thoughtfully, reminding me she's a psychologist. "Intense."

I nearly choke on my water. If she only knew exactly how *intense* Rylan Collings really is.

"He's good captain," I manage, aiming for casual. "He's good at keeping the team focused."

"Hmm." Mom nods. She's always been incredibly good at reading people. Goes with the territory, I guess. "And you're settling in okay? Making friends?"

Before I can answer, movement by the door catches my eye. My heart nearly stops.

Standing at the front of the restaurant is Rylan, with two guys who must be Aleks Warren and Ben Jacobs, the friends he'd mentioned meeting tonight. He'd told me earlier that Aleks used to be the Sasquatch's equipment manager before taking an assistant GM position with the Bears when his partner, a neurosurgeon, got some fancy research job in Boston. But seeing him *here*, in one of my family's favorite restaurants, while my psychologist mother is sitting across from me, analyzing our 'interesting team dynamic'... *Jesus Christ.*

I nearly knock over my water glass as memories of last night crash through my brain. *Not* thoughts I want to have while sitting next to my highly perceptive mother.

"Jamie?" Mom's voice breaks through my daze. "Are you listening, honey?"

"Sorry, just..." I tear my eyes away from Rylan. "Thought I saw someone I know."

But Mom's already turning to look, *because of course she is*, and her face lights up. "Oh! Isn't that your team captain? We should invite them to join us! There's plenty of room."

"Mom, no, that's not—"

But she's already waving. The flash of panic in Rylan's eyes probably mirrors my own before his mask slides back into place.

Well, so much for keeping our distance in public.

Chapter 29

RYLAN

For fuck's sake. Of all the restaurants in Boston...

I freeze mid-step, causing Ben to bump into me from behind.

Jamie's family takes up the corner table like they own it, radiating that casual confidence that comes from old money and Ivy League degrees. His father's got reading glasses perched on his nose. His brother, the neurosurgeon—because of course he's a fucking *neurosurgeon*—is gesturing animatedly about something while his lawyer sister nods. And there's Jamie, looking unfairly gorgeous in his post-game suit, wearing that deer-in-headlights expression as his elegantly dressed mother spots us and waves us over with an enthusiastic smile.

My carefully constructed walls start crumbling at the edges from just watching them together, their easy affection and inside jokes. Everything I lost after my

Mom and Nick died. Everything I've convinced myself I don't need anymore.

"Over here!" Alexandra calls, waving excitedly, somehow managing to look both elegant and enthusiastic. "Please, you must join us!"

"Dude," Aleks mutters behind me. "Is that Jamie Pirelli's mom trying to wave us over?"

"Apparently," I paste on what I hope passes for a professional smile.

"Wait, is that Adam Pirelli?" Ben says suddenly. Because, of course, they know each other. They're both brilliant neurosurgeons. Which means there's officially no escape from this dinner.

Jamie's mom is already heading in our direction with the same effortless grace Jamie has on the ice. "I'm Alexandra Pirelli," she says warmly, extending her hand. "You must be Rylan Collings. It's so nice to meet you in person."

Her smile is so genuine it hurts. When was the last time someone's mom, other than maybe Jenny Tremblay, looked at me like that? Like I matter beyond my stats and captain's letter.

Over her shoulder, Jamie looks like he wants to slide under the table. I know exactly how he feels.

"It's nice to meet you too, Mrs. Pirelli."

"Alexandra, please." Her smile reaches her eyes, creating tiny laugh lines. "And you must all join us. There's plenty of room."

"Oh, we wouldn't want to intru—"

"Dr. Ben Jacobs?" Jamie's brother interrupts, recognition lighting his face. "I just read the paper you published. It was brilliant."

"Dr. Adam Pirelli," Ben grins, extending his hand. "Great to see you again."

Alexandra's smile widens. "Well, this is wonderful! Joseph, dear, make room, please. We need to grab more chairs."

Jamie's father smiles up at us. "Fair warning, gentlemen. When Alexandra decides you're joining us for dinner, resistance is futile. It's best to surrender gracefully."

Before I know it, we're swept into their orbit. The waitstaff appears as if summoned by magic, pushing tables together and producing extra place settings. Somehow, I end up beside Jamie. Our knees brush briefly under the table before I can shift away. His mom settles directly across from me, her keen but friendly eyes missing nothing.

"They do a butternut squash ravioli here that's amazing," she says, smoothly steering the conversation as Ben and Adam launch into rapid-fire medical talk that might as well be Finnish. "Though Jamie tells me you're quite particular about your pre-game meals?"

"I, uh..." I focus on unfolding my napkin with military precision. "Yeah, I try to stick to a routine."

"Smart," Jamie's sister, Lola, chimes in. "I do the same before big court cases. Though I doubt my protein bar and triple espresso breakfast would cut it for professional athletes."

"You'd be surprised," Jamie says, with a grin. "There are guys who survive on nothing but coffee and determination during playoff runs."

"Jamie Alexander," Alexandra scolds, but her eyes are twinkling. "Don't be ridiculous!"

Jamie grins behind his water glass, clearly enjoying pushing his mom's buttons a little.

"So, Rylan, Jamie tells me you've been helping him adjust to Seattle?"

"Well, sure. The entire team helps new players settle in," I say carefully. Under the table, Jamie's knee brushes mine again. This time, I can't make myself pull away.

"Still, it must be nice to have someone looking out for you," she says to Jamie, but her eyes never leave my face. "Especially given your terrible experience in Florida."

The protective surge that hits me is instant and overwhelming. "Jamie's been a great addition to the Sasquatch," I say, maybe a little too forcefully. "It was Florida's loss when they traded him."

I glance over to find Jamie staring at me, a soft expression on his face that makes my chest ache. Alexandra's smile could power the city of Boston.

"Well," she says finally. "I'm glad he has such a passionate advocate in his corner."

Later, when the server appears beside her, she eyeballs my nearly empty plate. "I know you're conscious about nutrition, but please tell me you'll order dessert?" Her eyes crinkle around the edges with her warm smile.

"Oh no, I'm fine." I straighten my silverware, avoiding her gentle concern. "Jamie wasn't kidding. I watch my intake pretty carefully."

"Mm." She smiles. "There's nothing we can tempt you with? I mean, the rest of us have all stuffed ourselves with pasta. I hate to see you missing out." It's been years since anyone fussed over what I eat, and her simple, motherly concern causes a lump to rise in my throat.

"Mom tends to get a little pushy around food. She claims it's how she shows love," Jamie says, shooting her a raised eyebrow.

"I know, I know. I'm a caretaker at heart, so it comes from a good place. But I'm sorry if I'm pushing too hard," she says, the smile still on her face. "I think it's partly the Italian in me. Food is a whole thing with us."

"Yeah, she's not kidding," Lola chimes in. "It's impossible to be on a diet around my mother." She grins as Alexandra waves her hand and rolls her eyes at her daughter.

"Diet culture! Don't even get me started! That's partly why we have such an issue with obesity in this country!" she says. "Speaking about food, though, we're all going to be in Seattle for Thanksgiving in a couple of weeks. What are your plans for the holiday, Rylan?"

The question sounds casual, but there's something in her eyes that suggests she already knows what my answer will be.

"Well, um," I adjust my water glass so it's in alignment with my plate. "We have a game the night before Thanksgiving, so..."

"You'll join us for dinner," she says, so naturally, it takes me a moment to process. "It's nothing fancy, just a family dinner at Jamie's apartment."

"Oh, I couldn't—"

"I insist." Her tone is gentle but brooks no argument. "No one should be alone on Thanksgiving."

"You should come," Jamie says from beside me. "Pirelli holiday dinners are always an adventure. My mom will try to analyze everyone's food choices for hidden psychological meaning."

"Jamie!" But Alexandra's laughing. "You're so ridiculous, I do no such thing!"

Jamie's expression is so soft, my heart flips. Under the table, he slides his hand onto my knee and squeezes gently. My heart stutters in my chest.

"Wow, um, okay then." My throat is tight. "Thank you. I'd like that."

CHAPTER 30

RYLAN

The wine bottle is heavy in my hands as I stand outside Jamie's door. I spent an hour at the wine shop, analyzing vintages with the same intensity I use for reviewing game tape. The clerk probably thought I was insane.

Deep breath. I've faced playoff elimination games with less anxiety than I'm feeling about this dinner, but this is different. This is Jamie's *family*.

The door swings before I can knock, and Jamie's there, wearing a soft sweater that makes his eyes impossibly blue. His curls are a little messy, like he's been running his hands through them.

"Early as always." He smiles as he rakes his eyes down my body. "My parents are stuck in traffic since, for some unknown reason, they rented an Airbnb on the opposite side of town." He rolls his eyes, but his tone is more amused than annoyed. "And the sibs won't be here for another hour, either." Lola and Adam, who were at the dinner in Boston, are in town with their parents, which means the only family member I haven't met is his brother Edward, the NASA scientist in Houston. Apparently, the space program doesn't take Thanksgiving off.

He glances down the hallway before pulling me inside. The door clicks shut, and we're alone in his space. His actual home, not another hotel room. He has books scattered everywhere, academic non-fiction mixed in with novels, spread across coffee tables and stacked on shelves. Family photos sit beside random hockey memorabilia, and quirky art covers the walls. His space is just like him: stylish with an underlying warmth that makes my chest ache.

"Here." I thrust the wine at him. "The wine store guy said the acidity should complement the—"

Jamie's fond laugh cuts me off. "You're adorable when you overthink things." He steps closer, right into my space. "We have at least forty-five minutes," he murmurs, eyes dropping to my mouth. "Any ideas on how to pass the time?"

"Jamie..." His name comes out rougher than intended. "We shouldn't..."

"Why not?" His fingers trail up my arm. "We're alone. And you look..." His eyes drag over me, heating my skin. "*Really* good in that sweater."

I should step back. But I don't.

"Fuck it," I mutter, pulling him into a kiss.

He makes a pleased sound against my mouth, backing me against his kitchen counter while my heart pounds in my chest.

"Been wanting to do this all week," he mumbles between kisses. "Do you have any idea how hard it is to watch you in the weight room and not touch?"

A breathless laugh escapes me. "I can imagine. I have to see you stretch after practice."

"Yeah?" His smile turns wicked. "Like what you see, captain?"

"You know I do, you menace." But I'm smiling too, letting myself relax into this moment. Into him.

At the sound of a key in the lock, we spring apart like startled teenagers caught making out.

"Jamie?" Alexandra's voice carries from the entryway. "Traffic wasn't as bad as we thought!"

Panic floods my system as I hastily straighten my sweater while Jamie runs a hand through his curls, trying to tame them.

"In the kitchen, Mom!" he calls, voice slightly strained. "Rylan just got here, too."

Alexandra appears in the doorway. Her eyes take in the scene: Jamie's mussed hair, my flushed face, the unopened wine on the counter, and something knowing crosses her expression.

Panic claws at the back of my throat. *Oh my god, she's going to suspect us.* But when I meet her eyes, there's no judgment in them. Only the same warm acceptance from when we met before.

"Perfect timing," she says smoothly. "Joseph's parking the car. Rylan, dear, would you mind helping Jamie with the appetizers while I freshen up?"

"Of course, Mrs—um Alexandra," I correct myself at her look.

As she disappears down the hall, Jamie lets out a shaky breath. "Well. That was..."

"Yeah." I glance at him. His lips are still swollen from our kisses, and something possessive flares in my chest.

A teasing smirk appears on his face as he reads my expression. Then, as footsteps approach, he says loudly, "Can you grab those crackers from the pantry?"

We fall into an easy rhythm in the kitchen as we wait for his brother and sister to arrive. At one point, I catch Alexandra watching us; her smile soft and understanding in a way that makes my throat tight.

For dinner, we squeeze around Jamie's cobbled-together dining setup, his regular table plus a card table, all covered by a tablecloth I'm pretty sure Alexandra brought. The space manages to feel cozy instead of crowded, and the conversation flows easily.

"So Seattle's your first American team?" Lola asks, leaning forward with interest. "After Montreal and Toronto, right?"

"Winnipeg too," I add. "For a couple of seasons between Montreal and Toronto."

"That's quite a journey," Alexandra says. "All those Canadian teams before coming here. How are you finding life in the U.S.?"

"Different," I admit. "Even after three years, some things still catch me off guard. Like Thanksgiving being in November instead of October."

Everyone chuckles at that.

"Well, we're certainly glad you ended up here," Alexandra says warmly.

Under the table, Jamie's foot presses against mine again. Grounding me like he always does.

As the meal ends, I find myself in the kitchen with Alexandra, clearing dishes while Jamie argues with his siblings about who pushed whom into the lake at their cabin one summer.

Her hand on my arm is gentle. "Rylan, I wanted to thank you for everything you've done for Jamie since he's been here. He's so much more himself than he ever was during his time with the Jaguars. He seems happier, and that's partly because of you. And the rest of the team, of course."

My heart nearly stops. "I, uh, the team has been—"

"You don't have to say anything." Her smile reminds me of Jamie's. "Just... Thank you. And I want you to know you're always welcome with us. Anytime."

It's such a simple offer, but it cracks something open inside my chest. Something that's been tightly sealed since losing half my family, leaving me alone with my dad's grief and anger. Since I learned that loving people means losing them.

I manage to nod. When I get back to the table, Jamie's expression is soft as he looks at me. And I like the way that makes me feel. Way too much.

As the evening winds down, the family gets ready to head out. Before they get out the door, Alexandra pulls me into a warm hug. "Thank you for sharing the holiday with us," she murmurs.

"Thank you for having me," I choke out, my voice rough.

She squeezes my arm one more time, her eyes knowing. "Take care of each other," she says softly, glancing between Jamie and me. Then, louder, "Joseph! Come on, darling."

They all say goodbye like my being here is a regular thing, like I belong at their family gatherings. Yet again, a lump appears in my throat.

Eventually, the door closes behind them. The sudden silence is heavy with all the things I'm trying *not* to feel.

"Hey." Jamie's voice is soft as he moves closer. "You okay?"

I nod, not trusting my voice. He reaches for me slowly, like he's afraid I might bolt. When I don't pull away, he wraps his arms around me from behind, pressing his face into my neck.

"Thank you," he murmurs. "For being here. For letting them take care of you."

"Jamie..." My voice breaks on his name.

"I know." He tightens his arms. "They can be a lot. But they mean it, you know. About you being welcome. About wanting you here."

Closing my eyes, I allow myself to lean back into him for a moment, unable to force myself away from his solid, reassuring warmth.

"Stay?" His voice is husky. "Please? Just... stay tonight? I... I don't want to let you go yet."

I should say no. It's way too risky. What if someone sees me leave tomorrow morning? Several guys from the team live around here. I shouldn't...

"Okay," I whisper, turning in his arms. "Okay."

His smile is soft and full of something that looks a lot like hope.

And for once, I let myself hope, too.

CHAPTER 31

JAMIE

A few days after Thanksgiving, my footsteps echo in the empty halls as I arrive at the rink stupidly early, unable to sleep. My hands shake as I tape my stick and there are still two hours before our optional morning skate.

A memory flashes into my mind: early morning practices down in Florida. The way Nathan Leblanc's casual "Hey, queer" replaced his once-friendly greetings. And of course, the way the locker room would go silent when anyone made a crack like that. Even the guys who weren't outright snickering would mysteriously become very absorbed in inspecting their gear.

Not even the lingering warmth of Thanksgiving with my family, of watching Rylan slowly let his walls down with them, can quite chase away the cold dread of facing my old team today.

"Thought I might find you here." Louis's voice breaks through the memory. He drops his bag with a thud. "Couldn't sleep either?"

"That obvious?" My tape job's a mess again. I rip it off and start over.

"Nah." Louis starts his own methodical gear prep. "I still find it hard to sleep the night before big games. Even though I'm getting so long in the tooth now."

I snort. "Well, at least I won't have any illusions that it will get easier over the years."

The locker room door opens again, and Charlie bounces in with way too much energy for this hour. He's holding a cup of coffee in each hand. "Brought reinforcements!" He holds one out to me. "Though you look like you've already had about twelve."

The coffee's exactly how I like it. These little gestures still catch me off guard, my teammates paying attention to each other, actually giving a shit, and lending support when someone needs it. It's like being in Bizzaro World when compared to my first three years in the league.

"Hey." Rylan's voice cuts through my doom spiral. "You're thinking too loud."

Heat crawls up my neck. Because yeah, I'm thinking about my shit experience with the Jaguars, but I'm also thinking about last night. His heated whispers in the dark of my room, the way he looked on his knees in front of me... Fuuuck. *Not the time, Pirelli. Not the time.*

"I'm good," I manage. But he sees right through it, like always.

"Sure you are." His voice is a perfect mix of a team captain's authority and something softer that's just for me. "Let's get you out there. Ice time's the best cure I know of for overthinking shit."

He's right, of course; being on the ice does help. There's something about the clean scrape of skates, the familiar rhythm of drills. Coach keeps it light, but my linemates stick close.

"Alright, wrap it up!" Coach's whistle pierces the air. "Good work, everyone."

I'm peeling off my practice jersey when Carson Wells appears in the doorway. "Pirelli. Got a minute?"

Rylan tenses beside me, but I try to reassure him with a smile. "Don't worry, I'm sure it's nothing."

But as I follow Carson out, I catch Rylan watching me, concern on his face. And fuck, that look seems to say he would take on my whole past if he could. And that might be more dangerous than anything the Jags throw at me.

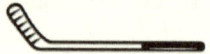

Carson Wells' office is all clean lines and views of Elliott Bay, but there's something in his expression that makes my throat tighten up when he gestures for me to take a chair by the windows. "How are you holding up?"

"I'm fine." The lie comes automatically. "Ready to play tonight."

"Jamie." His use of my first name gets my attention. "You don't have to be fine." He leans forward, his eyes boring into mine. "I saw what was going on in Florida. And so did Coach Shaw. Your teammates let you down, big time, and the fact that management looked the other way is almost worse."

My hands clench into fists. "Maybe, but I handled it poorly," I admit. "I gave them exactly what they wanted. I turned into a distraction."

"You were barely twenty years old." Carson's voice cuts through my self-recrimination. "And you were trying to deal with harassment from people who should have protected you. But you showed up every night and worked. You managed to put up points and tried to connect with teammates who didn't have your back."

"Not well enough," I mutter, remembering the headlines.

"Well enough to catch my attention." There's something fierce in Carson's tone now.

I blink hard, surprised by the emotion in his voice.

"This isn't Florida," he continues more gently.

"No," I agree quietly. "Down there... One of the first guys to welcome me was Nathan Leblanc. He made this big show of not caring that I was bi. We hung out a lot those first few months."

"But?"

"Something changed." I run a hand through my hair, remembering the frustration I felt and how confused I was. "Almost overnight. One day we were grabbing coffee, talking about music, normal shit. The next, he was..." I swallow hard. "He started making comments. Little digs at first, then bigger ones.

By the end, he was leading the charge to make my life hell."

"I'm sorry, that must have been rough," Carson says.

"Yeah. That was almost worse than the other stuff. The open harassment was easier to understand... I mean, some people are just assholes. But I never figured out why someone who'd been a friend suddenly hated me."

"Well, I'm happy things are better now. The entire organization supports you here, and I hope you can feel that. Your teammates value you, and I don't mean just your hockey skills, but *you*. The way you help the rookies, the way you've embraced our team culture. Your work ethic and positive attitude. You've shown us who you are in a short time, Pirelli. You should be proud of yourself. You're a big asset to this team and I'm happy as hell that I took the risk to bring you to the Sasquatch."

"Thanks, Carson." My voice comes out rough.

He nods once as he gets up from his chair. "Show those fucks what they lost tonight."

When I get back to the locker room, Rylan's waiting for me. He's leaning against the wall, all casual-like, but just seeing him settles something inside me.

"Everything okay?" he asks quietly.

I look at him—really look at him. This man who has become so much more than just a teammate. Who makes me believe I deserve more than what I had before.

"Yeah," I say with a small smile. "Everything's okay."

CHAPTER 32

JAMIE

The familiar pulse of pre-game warmups thrums through me as we take the ice. Normally, I love the anticipation, but tonight, my stomach is churning unpleasantly. Florida's dark jerseys blur in my peripheral vision because I refuse to give them my attention until I have to, focusing instead on my team.

"Don't let them in your head," Louis told me earlier, his usual playful demeanor replaced by fierce protectiveness. "They're just another team now. You're one of us."

His words echo as I send another puck top shelf, earning appreciative taps from Charlie and Gino. Even Austin's usual gruff energy feels supportive, like he's daring anyone to mess with me. The team forms a loose circle around me during warmups. It's nothing obvious, but I'm never left exposed.

Nathan Leblanc is staring me down from the visitors' bench, his glare like a physical weight on my chest. But I refuse to look his way. Fucker's not worth it. My attention stays where it belongs: on the crisp passes Rylan keeps sending me. We're on the same wavelength tonight, our connection smooth and instinctive, like we've been playing together for years instead of months.

The memory of my first NHL goal slams into me: Nate throwing his arm around my shoulders, bellowing proudly, "That's my rookie!" while the guys mobbed us both. What should be a fond memory is tainted now, though, poisoned by how fast he turned on me after that. *Shit, my head's not in it.* An easy pass from Gagnon sails right past me. *Goddamnit.*

"Hey." Rylan appears beside me, close enough that I can hear him over the crowd noise. "Stay with me."

The quiet command in his voice centers me. His eyes hold mine for a moment, and his quiet confidence steadies me.

"We're ready." He says as we line up for the opening faceoff.

When the puck drops, everything else falls away.

During the first shift, Leblanc tries to line me up along the boards, but Santucci, our big, grouchy defenseman, appears out of nowhere, a wall of muscle forcing him to pull up. The message is clear: *not here, motherfuckers. Not in our house.*

We go up 1-0 early on Charlie's wrister from the slot. The crowd roars as we celebrate, and my teammates' bodies form a protective circle around me during the celly. I catch Vladimir Belov sneering from Florida's bench, but his hatred is distant and meaningless now.

During the second period things get chippy. Every hit is harder than necessary, and every scrum ends with an "accidental" elbow or a borderline high stick. Leblanc shadows me constantly, muttering taunts just quiet enough the officials can't hear.

"Hey, Pirelli, found another straight guy to corrupt, eh?"

I grit my teeth and keep skating. *Let that shit roll off. Water off a duck's back.* I'm not that same nervous kid trying to prove himself anymore.

The puck finds me in the neutral zone while Rylan breaks up the left side. Pure instinct takes over. No need to look; I know where he'll be. The pass connects perfectly, but before I can follow the play, Leblanc catches me with a late hit.

"Fucking fairy," he spits as I pick myself up.

Austin Coté appears out of nowhere, getting right up in Nathan's face. "Do it again, Leblanc," he growls. "See what happens."

The refs separate them, but something's shifted. Every Sasquatch player is on fire now, fueled by righteous anger. My team rallies around me in a way I never dreamed could happen in this league, even a year ago.

Heading into the third, we're tied 2-2. Coach's intermission speech is simple: "Play our game. Show them what we're made of, boys. They're in our barn; give 'em a lesson in Sasquatch hockey."

Rylan catches my eye, sending me a subtle up nod. We both know what's at stake here.

Back out on the ice, everything clicks. Our line's flying, connecting on plays that shouldn't even be possible. The Jags keep trying to get under my skin, but I focus on Rylan and the way we seem to read each other's minds.

With three minutes left, their defensemen are all over me, but they don't know how Rylan and I work together. One look, one subtle head tilt, and we're in perfect sync.

The goal is perfect. Rylan draws both defenders to him, then slides the puck right to me, through a gap that shouldn't exist. I one-time it, top shelf, right over their goalie's shoulder. The red lamp lights, the horn sounds, and the crowd explodes.

My teammates pile on, and for just a moment, I let myself hold on to Rylan longer than strictly necessary. In the chaos, no one notices. But I catch Leblanc's narrowed eyes focused on us as we head back to our bench.

The final minute is pure adrenaline. Florida pulls their goalie, sending six attackers our way, but Lou stands on his head, denying every last shot. When the final horn sounds, the relief hits me so hard that my knees almost buckle.

"Fucking brilliant!" Charlie screeches, crashing into me with a huge grin on his freckled face. The rest of the team follows, and through the crowd, I catch Rylan's eyes. His captain's mask is firmly in place, but his expression is full of pride, relief, and something deeper. It's a look that fills my gut with a delicious, liquid warmth.

The locker room buzzes with victory energy. I can't stop grinning, high on the win and the way we came together as a team.

"Three fucking stars tonight, baby!" Charlie's practically bouncing as he strips off his gear. "First star Pirelli, showing those Florida fucks what they lost!"

Louis tosses a towel at my head. "Hit the shower, hotshot. You stink of victory and ball sweat."

Standing under the hot water, I revel in the triumph, and it feels fucking amazing. It's more than winning the game, it's what this win means for me both as a player and a person. It means Florida's bullshit couldn't break me. They tried, but I found something better, something real. I found a team that has my back, a place where I feel like I belong. Like it might be home.

"Drinks," Gino Santucci announces. "First round's on me. No arguments."

A cheer goes up just as Rylan strides back into the locker area, fresh from the showers with only a towel wrapped around his waist. My mouth literally waters as my eyes trace the perfect lines of his shoulders and the way his torso narrows into his trim waist before getting to his perfect, incredible ass.

Jesus fucking Christ, I need to be careful. Probably wouldn't be great for anyone if I got caught eye-fucking our captain. But at this moment, riding this high, I can't find a good reason to care.

"Proper   celebration   required," Charlie agrees. "Those twats can drink alone tonight."

I catch Rylan sneaking glances at me as he methodically packs his gear. There's heat in his gaze that has nothing to do with the game.

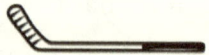

Bigfoot's Sin Bin, the new hockey bar by the arena, is packed when we arrive, the victory drawing Sasquatch fans like moths to flame. Charlie's already commandeered the corner, regaling anyone within earshot with a play-by-play of my game-winner. My skin is buzzing with leftover adrenaline from the win. And from Rylan's proximity on the other side of our table.

He's doing that controlled-captain thing, one hand wrapped around his beer bottle, nodding at something Santucci's saying. But his eyes keep finding me, and I like it a little too much.

"To Pirelli!" Charlie raises his glass, and the entire team joins in. Warmth floods my chest that has nothing to do with alcohol. This—this right here is what I never had with the Jaguars. Real teammates. Real friendship.

The puck bunnies find us fast, like they always do after a win. A leggy blonde in a cropped Sasquatch jersey presses against my side for a selfie, and I slip into autopilot charm mode: easy smiles and harmless flirtation. But in my peripheral vision, Rylan's shoulders are rigid, his jaw tight. When another woman, this one in painted-on jeans, runs her fingers down my arm, his knuckles go white around his beer bottle.

Fuck. I should stop. I know I'm playing with fire here, but I'm becoming addicted to seeing that crack in Rylan's careful control. About knowing he wants to stake his claim on me, even if he can't.

"Such a team player now."

Leblanc's voice cuts through my buzz. He's been lurking over by the bar, his eyes moving between me and Rylan for most of the night, but I've been determined to ignore him. What the hell is he even doing here, hanging out by himself at our victory celebration? It's creepy as fuck. My stomach knots.

Louis materializes beside me, radiating his laid-back goalie energy. "Hey, Leblanc. Still bitter about those goals I stole from you? You might wanna work on that wrist shot; I was reading you like a kid's book tonight."

Nathan's face darkens, but he slinks away.

"Another round!" Charlie announces, already weaving toward the bar. He stumbles, catching himself on Rylan's shoulder. Our captain steadies him with practiced ease, but his eyes find mine across the table. The heat in them makes my breath catch.

I should leave. Should make an excuse and get out before Leblanc picks up on anything else. But then Rylan shifts, his knee bumping mine under the table. The contact is brief, but electricity zings through my whole body.

This thing between us is scary as fuck. Rylan might *never* be ready to acknowledge us publicly. And I won't be able to hide forever; that's just not who I am. But fuck, when he looks at me like that...

The team starts breaking up naturally as midnight approaches. I hang back, letting the others file out first. Rylan does the same, maintaining careful distance. But I feel Nathan watching from his corner, that calculating look still on his face.

Outside, everyone splits up, with some guys ordering Ubers while others head toward their cars. I start toward my building, but Rylan catches my arm. His touch is casual, nothing anyone would notice, but it burns through my jacket.

"My place," he says quietly, not quite meeting my eyes. "It's closer."

Holy shit. My heart slams against my ribs. I've never been to Rylan's apartment. He treats it like his fortress of solitude, never inviting anyone over, as far as I know, and I wasn't sure he was ever going to let me behind that wall.

"You sure?" I ask, giving him an out.

He finally looks at me fully, and holy fuck, the raw *want* in his eyes makes me forget about Nathan Leblanc, about being careful, about everything except getting him alone. *Right. Fucking. Now.*

"Yeah," he says roughly. "I'm sure."

CHAPTER 33

RYLAN

M y hands shake as I unlock my door. I don't bring people here. Ever. This space is mine alone. It's my sanctuary, my fortress against the world. But tonight, watching Jamie step through the door feels... right.

He moves through my carefully ordered space like a force of nature, all golden curls and casual grace. His presence fills up the emptiness I've never let myself acknowledge, making everything feel more alive.

"So this is Captain Collings' lair?" A hint of fond amusement colors his voice as he takes in the precise alignment of my shoes and the methodically arranged hockey memorabilia. "It's very... you."

The soft laugh that escapes him makes my chest tight. I should feel exposed and uncomfortable having him here. Instead, for some reason, I have an intense need to show him everything.

I swallow hard, stepping closer. "Jamie." My voice comes out rough, and his eyes flicker up, a spark of heat in their blue depths.

"Yeah?" He takes the final step that closes the distance between us, and the warmth of his body sends a shiver down my spine. His fingers brush my jaw, and the gentle touch burns through all my control.

"I don't..." The words stick in my throat. I've never been good at asking for what I want. But Jamie waits, patient and steady, his thumb tracing slow circles on my skin.

"What do you want, Ry?" he whispers, his voice dropping to that low register that makes my cock twitch.

I trail my hands up his chest, feeling the steady beat of his heart under my palms. "I don't want to hide anymore. Not with you."

His intake of breath is sharp. "Show me," he urges, and then his mouth is on mine.

It's different from our previous encounters. This is slower, deeper, like he's trying to memorize every breath, every touch. My back hits the wall, and I groan, pulling him flush against me. Every curve of his body molds to mine, and fuck, I'm already hard, already aching for him.

His lips move to my neck, his teeth grazing my pulse point. "Been thinking about this all night," he murmurs. "The way you looked after scoring that goal... fuck, Ry, wanted to take you right there in the locker room."

My brain won't form a response, so I just tangle my hands in his hair, holding him close. His thigh slides between mine, making me buck my hips involuntarily as I seek more friction. "Bedroom," I manage. "Now."

He pulls back just enough to meet my eyes, and Christ, the heat in his gaze steals my breath. "You sure?"

Instead of answering, I grab his hand and drag him down the hall. When we reach my bedroom, the glow from the streetlights filters through the blinds, casting Jamie in a warm light that makes his curls look like a halo. He looks almost otherworldly, and for a moment, I forget how to breathe.

His hands slip under my shirt, and I gasp at the contact. His palms are hot against my skin, leaving trails of fire as they map every muscle. "God, you're gorgeous," he breathes, pushing my shirt up. "Been driving me crazy all night, watching you move on the ice."

I lift my arms, letting him strip off my shirt. For once, the careful way I usually fold my clothes doesn't even cross my mind—not with Jamie's mouth trailing down my neck, his teeth scraping lightly over my collarbone. His stubble rasps against my sensitive skin, sending sparks of pleasure straight to my cock.

"Jamie," I gasp when his tongue finds my nipple. I fist my hands in his curls, torn between pulling him closer and pushing him away. It's too much but not enough. It's everything at once.

"Love the sounds you make," he murmurs against my skin. His teeth graze my nipple, and my hips buck involuntarily. "Love watching you lose control." He slides his big hands down to grip my ass, pulling me against him. The friction makes me whimper. "You like that? Let me hear you, baby."

The pet name does something to my chest, making me feel both vulnerable and cherished. I tug at his shirt, suddenly desperate to feel his skin against mine. "Off. I need to feel you."

He strips his shirt off in one fluid motion, and fuck, he's beautiful. I've seen him shirtless countless times in the locker room, but this is different. This is mine. My hands shake as I trace the defined muscles of his chest, following the trail of golden hair that disappears into his jeans.

"See something you like?" His voice is pure sin, and when I look up, his blue eyes are dark with desire. He catches my wandering hands, bringing them to his lips to kiss my palms. "Tell me what you want, Ry. Want to hear you say it."

My careful control splinters. "You. Want you inside me." The words come out desperate and needy. "Please, Jamie."

"Fuck, baby." He captures my mouth in a searing kiss, walking me backward until my knees hit the bed. "Love when you beg for me."

His weight presses me into the mattress, and Christ, the feeling of skin on skin is overwhelming. He kisses down my chest, taking his time, like he's mapping every inch of me. When he reaches the waistband of my jeans, he looks up through those curls, and the sight nearly makes me come right there.

"These need to go," he growls, making quick work of the button and zipper. My hips lift automatically as he strips off my jeans and boxers together. Usually,

I'd fold them, but right now, I don't care if they end up wrinkled on the floor. Not when Jamie's looking at me like he wants to devour me.

"Gorgeous," he breathes, pressing open-mouthed kisses along my inner thighs. His stubble leaves a burning trail on my sensitive skin. "So fucking perfect for me."

His tongue traces the crease where my thigh meets my hip, deliberately avoiding where I need him most. I writhe under him, forgetting all about control, about maintaining composure. "Jamie, please..."

"Please what?" His breath ghosts over my cock, making me shudder. "Tell me what you need, baby. Want to hear you say it."

The words tear from my throat, raw and desperate. "Your mouth. Please, Jamie, I need..."

"Yeah?" He grins up at me, wicked and playful. "Like this?" His tongue drags up the length of my cock, and my back arches off the bed.

"Fuck!" I fist the sheets—my perfectly made bed becoming as disheveled as my thoughts.

"God, look at you," he murmurs, wrapping one big hand around my base. "Always so controlled, so put together. I love seeing you fall apart for me."

When he finally takes me into his mouth, my world narrows to pure sensation—the wet heat of his mouth, the slight scrape of his teeth, the vibration of his moan around me. His curls are like silk between my fingers as I fight not to thrust up.

"Jamie, Jamie, I can't..." The words dissolve into desperate sounds as he swallows me deeper.

He pulls off with an obscene pop. "I want to be inside you when you come," he says, his voice rough. "Want to feel you fall apart around me. Where's your lube, baby?"

"Bedside drawer," I manage. "Left side. Everything's organized by—" My words cut off in a gasp as he nips at my inner thigh.

"Of course it is," he chuckles. "I would expect nothing less."

JAMIE

The soft laugh that escapes him at my teasing makes my heart clench. Even now, flushed and desperate beneath me, he's meticulously organized. I find the lube exactly where he said, along with several boxes of condoms arranged by brand. Jesus Christ, he's going to be the death of me.

"Been thinking about this since San Diego," I murmur, coating my fingers. "The way you looked that night, letting go for me." I press soft kisses up his inner thigh as I circle his rim with one finger. "But this is different. Tonight, you're mine. All mine."

His breath hitches as I press just the tip of my finger inside him. "Jamie..."

He wiggles against me, desperately trying to get me to push into his body faster.

"Shhhh, baby, we need to go slow. I don't want to hurt you."

"You won't," he gasps. "I have... um... I have toys that I use."

I pull back to stare at him, my eyebrows shooting up. *Holy fuck.* The image of my perfectly controlled captain fucking himself with a dildo... My cock throbs painfully. "Jesus Christ, you're just full of surprises, aren't you?"

A flush spreads down his chest, but the glint in his eye makes my mouth water. "You have no idea."

"Fuck, baby," I groan, pressing my finger deeper. "Tell me about these toys. Do you think about me when you use them?"

His breath hitches as I work him open. "Yes," he admits, and Christ, the way he blushes even as he pushes back against my hand... "Ever since San Diego. Think about your cock while I..."

"While you what?" I add a second finger, curling them just right. "Tell me, Ry. I want to hear all your dirty secrets."

"While I fuck myself," he gasps. "Imagining it's you."

Jesus fucking Christ. This perfectly controlled, buttoned-up man has been fucking himself thinking about me. I press my forehead against his thigh, trying to maintain some control of my own. "You're going to kill me, you know that?"

His laugh turns into a moan as I curl my fingers again, brushing against that spot inside him. "Jamie, please. Need more."

"Yeah?" I add a third finger, loving how easily he opens for me. "Look at you, taking my fingers so well. Bet you practiced this, didn't you? Got yourself all ready, hoping I'd take you home tonight?"

The sound he makes is absolutely filthy. "Yes," he admits. "This morning..."

"Fuuuuuck," I groan. The image of him prepping himself, thinking about tonight. "That's so hot. Did you come thinking about my cock?"

"N-no," he gasps, grinding down on my fingers. "Wanted to wait. Wanted... wanted to come on your cock."

"Jesus fucking Christ." My control snaps. I withdraw my fingers, fumbling for a condom. He reaches out to stop me, his hands surprisingly steady.

"Let me," he says. The sight of him methodically tearing open the packet with his teeth is one of the hottest things I've ever seen. He rolls it down my length with precise movements that make my eyes roll back in my head.

"Rylan," I groan as he strokes me, spreading lube over my length. "Need to be inside you. Now."

He lies back, pulling me with him, and I have to stop for a moment to take him in. His usual perfect composure is nowhere to be found. His hair is messed up from my fingers, his lips swollen from my kisses, and his chest is flushed and heaving. He's the most beautiful thing I've ever seen.

"Jamie," he whimpers, wrapping those strong thighs around my waist. "Please."

I line myself up, pressing just the tip inside him. "Look at me. Want to see your face when I fill you up."

His eyes lock with mine as I push in slowly. "Fuck," he gasps, his fingers digging into my shoulders. "So big..."

"That's it, baby," I murmur, sinking deeper into his tight heat. "Taking me so perfectly. Just like you do everything else."

His back arches as I bottom out, a broken sound escaping him. "Jamie, please... need you to move."

"Yeah?" I roll my hips slowly, drinking in every gasp and shudder. "Like this? Or harder?" I snap my hips forward, making him cry out. "Tell me what you need. Want to make it so good for you."

"Harder," he begs, his usual measured tone completely gone. "Want to feel you tomorrow. Want... want to remember this every time I move."

"Fuck." I grab his hips, adjusting the angle until I find that spot that makes him see stars. "Like this? Want everyone to know you're mine? That their perfect captain lets me wreck him?"

"Yes," he moans, meeting every thrust. "Yours. Only yours."

His confession drives me wild. I lean down to capture his mouth, swallowing his desperate sounds as I fuck into him harder. One of his hands tangles in my curls while the other claws at my back, and the sting pushes me closer to the edge.

"Touch yourself for me, baby," I pant against his mouth. "Want to watch you fall apart."

His hand shakes as he wraps it around himself, and holy fuck, the sight of him stroking himself while I'm buried deep inside him... "Jamie, I'm close..."

"Yeah?" I slow my thrusts, making them deeper, harder. "You gonna come for me? Show me how good I make you feel?"

He nods frantically, his rhythm faltering as he gets closer. His other hand is still twisted in my curls, and the way he pulls makes electricity shoot down my spine.

"Come on, Rylan," I urge, angling my hips to hit that perfect spot. "Let go for me. Want to feel you come around my cock."

His whole body tenses, his back arching beautifully. "Jamie, I... fuck, I'm..."

"That's it, baby. Come for me."

He shatters with a cry, clenching around me so hard I see stars. The sight of him completely undone, muscles trembling, face flushed with pleasure, sends me right over the edge after him.

I collapse onto him, both of us trembling and gasping. He runs his hands gently up and down my sweaty back as we catch our breath, and the tender gesture makes my chest tight.

"Holy fuck," I manage finally, pressing lazy kisses along his jaw. "You're incredible."

He makes a quiet sound, turning his face into my neck. I can feel his heart still racing where our chests are pressed together. Carefully, I start to pull out, but his legs tighten around me.

"Stay inside me," he whispers. "Just... just for a minute."

Something about the vulnerability in his voice makes my throat tight. "Yeah, baby. I've got you."

We lie there, trading soft kisses until my softening cock begins to slide out of him. I press a kiss to his forehead, when he winces slightly. "Let me clean you up," I murmur.

He nods, looking adorably dazed. When I return with a warm washcloth, he's fighting to keep his eyes open. He's completely blissed out, and knowing I did that to him causes something possessive to unfurl in my chest.

I clean him up carefully, unable to resist pressing soft kisses to the marks I left on his thighs. "You good?"

"Mmm." He tugs me down next to him, immediately curling into my side. It's such an unguarded gesture, so different from his usual careful distance, that my heart trips over itself in my chest.

"Your sheets are a mess," I tease softly, running my fingers through his sweat-damp hair.

"Don't care," he mumbles against my chest. "Can wash them tomorrow."

I press a kiss to his temple, savoring this rare moment of him letting go of his perfect control. "I love seeing you like this."

His only response is a contented hum as he drifts off to sleep, completely trusting in my arms.

CHAPTER 34

RYLAN

Early morning sunlight filters through my bedroom windows, catching on Jamie's blonde hair where his head rests on my chest. Everything feels soft and hazy with the afterglow. His mouth was so perfect on me just minutes ago, and I'm still floating in that space where nothing exists except us.

"Stop thinking so loud," Jamie mumbles against my skin, pressing a lazy kiss to my collarbone. "It's too early for your brain to be working this hard."

I run my fingers through his messy curls, allowing myself this moment of pure contentment. "Just wondering how you got so good at that."

He props himself up on one elbow, grinning. "Natural talent. Though I'm happy to demonstrate again if you need more evidence."

My phone buzzes on the nightstand before I can respond. I reach for it automatically, the habit left over from when I was constantly worrying about my dad. But I freeze when I see the caller ID.

"Declan Summers?" Jamie reads it upside down, his playful expression shifting to concern. "What does he want this early?"

Sports reporters don't call at 7 AM unless something's going on. My hand shakes as I answer.

"Collings."

"Rylan." Declan's voice is tight and professional. "Sorry to call so early, but... you need to hear this. I got a strange call last night. From Nathan Leblanc."

My blood runs cold. Jamie must see something in my face because he sits up, all traces of morning laziness gone.

"What kind of call?" I manage, proud of how steady my voice sounds.

"He claims he has..." Declan pauses, clearing his throat. "Compromising information about you and Pirelli. Says he saw something physical happen between you at the bar last night. He's shopping the story around."

The room spins. Jamie's hand finds my shoulder, trying to ground me, but I barely feel it.

"Rylan?" Declan's voice softens. "I won't run with this. I would never out someone. But... someone will. This kind of story, especially with you two playing like you have been lately... sex sells. And gay sex sells even better, as fucked up as that is."

I can't breathe. Can't think. Can't...

"Thanks for the heads up," I hear myself say, my voice on autopilot.

"Yeah." Declan sighs. "For what it's worth, Rylan... I don't know if it's true or not, but either way, I'm sorry. People are dicks."

"Yeah, thanks," I say robotically, before ending the call.

The call ends. Jamie's still watching me, those blue eyes full of concern.

"Ry?" he says softly. "Talk to me. What's going on?"

But panic is already clawing up my throat, threatening to choke me. Everything I've built, the life I've protected so fucking carefully...

"Nathan Leblanc knows," I manage. "He called Declan. He's telling reporters he saw something between us. It's going to get out, Jamie. No matter what. Declan won't run with it, but someone will. Even if it's just some shitty blogger. "

Jamie's face goes pale. "What exactly did he see?"

"Does it matter?" My voice comes out harsh as I push myself up, needing to move. "He saw enough. We were practically eye-fucking each other all night. Maybe he followed us, or—"

"Hey." Jamie reaches for me, but I flinch away. I can't handle his touch right now. Not when everything's falling apart.

"We have to deny it," I say, pacing back and forth, running my hand through my hair. My carefully organized bedroom suddenly feels like a fishbowl. I'm too exposed here. But there's nowhere else in the world I feel safe. "We have to say it's just a dirty rumor. We're just teammates, and they're targeting you because you're one of the few out players in the league..."

"Rylan." Jamie's voice is so gentle it hurts. "Maybe... maybe this isn't the worst thing. Maybe it's time to—"

"Time to what?" I spin to face him. "Time to destroy everything I've built? Time to let my father find out from some trashy website that his only remaining family member is— ?" I cut myself off, unable to even say the fucking word. *God, I'm a pathetic piece of shit. What a fucking coward.*

"That's not—"

"You don't understand." My hands are shaking so hard I have to clench them into fists to stop. "You're already out. You've dealt with this. But I'm the team captain. I have responsibilities. I can't—"

"I'll deny it," Jamie cuts in quietly. "If that's what you want. I'll say Nathan's lying, that there's nothing between us."

His simple offer breaks something inside me. Because, of course, he would do that. Of course, he'd offer to go back into the closet for me. He's volunteering to hide himself so I can protect my carefully constructed life, even though it's hurting him.

"Jamie..." My voice cracks.

"Hey." He stands, moving toward me slowly like I'm a spooked animal. "Whatever you need. We'll handle this however you want."

But I can see what it costs him to make that offer. The hurt in his eyes is unmistakable.

"I can't—" My breath is coming too fast, and the room is spinning. "I need to think. I need..."

"Okay, okay, it's going to be okay." He steps back. "What do you need from me?"

You, I want to say. *Just you. Always you.* But the words stick in my throat.

I collapse onto my bed, hunched over with my elbows on my knees, holding my head in my hands. *Fuck, I need air.* "I need to be alone... I can't..."

Understanding floods his face, followed quickly by a flash of raw pain, before his expression closes off, his lips forming into a thin line. "Okay," he says again, but there's an edge to his voice. "I'll go."

I force myself to meet his eyes. "I'm sorry." I choke out, unable to come up with anything more meaningful to say.

I watch as he gathers his clothes, his every movement careful and controlled like he's trying not to spook me any further. At the door, he pauses.

"Just... remember you don't *have* to be alone anymore, Rylan."

I can't speak. Can barely breathe. He nods once when I don't respond, and then he's gone.

The quiet of my apartment closes in, suffocating me, as the door closes behind him. I sink to the floor with my back against my perfect designer sofa, and try to remember how to breathe.

CHAPTER 35

JAMIE

My stick feels heavy as I step onto the ice for practice, weighed down by everything unsaid. Rylan's already out there, of course, the perfect captain, acting like nothing's wrong. Like he didn't shatter both our hearts this morning.

"Looking a little rough, Pirelli," Charlie comments as I join the warm-up laps. "Big celebration last night?"

"Something like that."

Louis gives me a sharp look as he skates past, too perceptive as always. But I focus on the ice, on my edges, on anything except how Rylan won't meet my eyes.

"First line!" Coach calls. "Let's see that chemistry from last night!"

My stomach lurches. Because even now, even with everything falling apart, our bodies know this dance. The puck finds me exactly where Rylan knew I'd be, his pass landing perfectly on my tape. Like always. Like nothing's changed.

Except everything's changed.

"Beautiful!" Coach yells as I bury it top shelf over Tanner's shoulder. "That's what I'm talking about!"

I risk a glance at Rylan, but his captain's mask is firmly in place. Only someone who's seen him fall apart, who's watched him let those walls down, would notice how his hands shake slightly.

"Again!" Coach demands.

We run the play over and over, each perfect connection feeling like a fresh wound.

"Pirelli!" Austin's sharp voice breaks through my spiral. "Head in the game!"

I've missed a pass—the first time that's happened in months. Rylan flinches slightly, so subtly I'm the only one who notices.

"Sorry," I mutter, retrieving the puck. "Won't happen again."

"Everything okay?" Louis asks quietly as we circle back. "You seem..."

"Fine." The lie tastes bitter. "Just tired."

His eyes flick between Rylan and me. "Right."

The rest of practice passes in a blur of barely contained emotion. Every time Rylan and I connect on a play, which is often, the rest of the team exchanges looks. They can tell something's off, even if they don't know what.

"Good work!" Coach calls finally. "Hit the showers."

My stomach drops. Rylan's shoulders tense almost imperceptibly.

In the locker room, the silence between Rylan and me feels deafening. We move through our usual routines, carefully maintaining our distance, but I can't stop stealing glances. Can't stop remembering how different this was yesterday, when everything felt possible.

"Jamie." Louis's voice is low as he appears beside me. "Whatever's going on..."

"Don't." My voice cracks slightly. "Please."

He squeezes my shoulder once, understanding.

"Heads up, guys." Riley appears in the doorway, a confused look on her face. "Media's getting pushy. They're asking about some weird rumor some blogger started."

"I'll handle it," Rylan cuts in smoothly, his captain's voice perfect and controlled. Like he didn't whisper my name as he came only a few hours ago.

"They're specifically asking for both you and Pirelli," Riley says carefully.

My eyes meet Rylan's across the room. For just a second, I see everything he's trying to hide—the fear, the pain, the desperate need to protect himself. Then his walls slam back up.

"Let's get this over with," he says professionally.

As we head toward the media scrum, I remember his words from this morning: *We have to deny it.*

My heart cracks a little more with each step.

The reporters descend before we even make it down the hallway. Their questions overlap, aggressive and hungry:

"Rylan, care to comment on rumors about your relationship with Pirelli?"

"Jamie, is this similar to situations in Florida?"

"How long has this been going on?"

"Sources suggest inappropriate conduct between teammates. Do you have any comment?"

My stomach churns, but I keep my media smile firmly in place. Next to me, Rylan is perfectly composed, of course. Every inch the responsible team captain. As always.

"I appreciate everyone's interest," Rylan says smoothly, his voice carrying that calm authority I find so hot. "But these rumors are completely unfounded. Pirelli is a talented hockey player and a valued teammate. Nothing more."

The words hit like body checks. *Nothing more. Nothing more. Nothing more.*

"But witnesses report seeing you two in compromising positions—"

"My relationship with Pirelli is purely professional." Rylan's tone could freeze hell. "Any suggestion otherwise is not only false but potentially damaging to team chemistry."

I force myself to nod, trying to look dismissive. But inside, I'm screaming. Because this isn't like what happened in Florida—this isn't malicious assholes spreading lies, just trying to hurt me. This is *real*. This is everything I've wanted since I first saw him.

And he's standing there calling it "unfounded."

"Jamie?" A reporter thrusts a mic in my face. "Any comment on these allegations?"

I open my mouth, but no sound comes out. Because what can I say? That watching Rylan deny us is killing me? That I understand why he's doing it, but it still feels like my heart's being ripped out of my chest?

"I think we've addressed this sufficiently," Rylan cuts in, his captain's authority brooking no argument. "Now, if you'll excuse us, we have team obligations."

As we turn to leave, I catch his expression cracking for just a fraction of a second. The pain in his eyes matches the ache in my chest.

But then his walls slam back up, and he's striding away from me, his every movement precise and controlled. Like he didn't just deny everything we could have been.

Like he didn't just break both our hearts.

Chapter 36

RYLAN

My bedroom is too goddamn quiet. The old digital clock on my bedside table glows 2:47 AM, its red numbers accusing. I can't stop seeing Jamie's face during that press conference. The flash of raw hurt in his eyes before he locked it away, covering it with a carefully blank expression when I said we were nothing more than teammates.

It was the same hurt I saw this morning when he offered to deny everything, to protect me, even though it would hurt him.

Sleep is impossible. Every time I close my eyes, I can see him in this same bed—golden and perfect in the morning light, telling me I didn't have to be alone anymore.

Except I made sure I was alone, didn't I? Did exactly what I always do—I push away anything that threatens my control. My carefully constructed life that's designed to make me feel safe. Only it's never felt quite so empty before.

Fuck.

I throw off the covers and head into my great room. My perfectly organized apartment is suffocating. Every precise angle, every carefully curated space feels like a distorted, fun-house reflection of me. It's all fake, this perfect control. Under this calm surface, I'm a fucking mess. A chaotic, ugly, cowardly mess.

My keys are in my hand before I make a conscious decision. Greg, the night custodian at the practice rink, knows me. It won't be the first time I've taken refuge on the ice in the middle of the night, and it probably won't be the last.

The drive to the practice rink is automatic, muscle memory taking over while my mind spins. I'm haunted by the look on Jamie's face. The way he just stood there and let me deny everything we could have been because he knew that's what I needed.

The building is dark except for the security lights, but my access card still works. Once I get to the Sasquatch rink, the familiar smell of ice and rubber flooring settles in my chest. This, at least, makes sense. This I understand.

Greg barely looks up from his cleaning cart, just gives me a small nod. He's used to my late-night visits by now, understands sometimes a player just needs ice time to think.

The locker room feels different at night—like the ghosts of past games linger in here, both the celebrations and the anger and disappointment. My footsteps echo as I head to my stall, the familiar motions of lacing up my skates providing small comfort. Every movement is precise and controlled, but it's never been so obvious that the control is only an illusion.

The ice gleams under the dimmed lights as I step out. Just me and this sheet of ice that's been my refuge for as long as I can remember. Nick and my dad taught me on our backyard rink and our small-town arena, but ice is ice. It doesn't matter where you are, or what's surrounding it, or even what's going on in my head. The sound of ice meeting metal when my skate blades make contact is always the same. It's like the soundtrack of my life.

"I don't know what the fuck I'm doing, Nick," I mutter under my breath. "What am I supposed to do?"

My skates cut clean lines across the fresh ice. No real pattern, just feeling the edge of my blades, the familiar resistance. The thing about my brother was that even though he was young when he died, he was wise as hell. My mom used to say he was an old soul. He never ran from anything, even when he was scared. And he never tried to be anyone other than who he was.

"You can't control everything, Ry," I can almost hear his voice. *"Sometimes you have to let go."*

A sound that's half laugh, half sob escapes me as I pick up speed. The cold air feels good in my lungs.

"Bit late for practice, isn't it?"

I nearly wipe out at Carson's voice. He's standing at the boards, coffee mug in his hand, watching me.

"Holy shit, you scared me," I say, forcing out a laugh.

"Mind if I join you for a bit?" he says with a wry smile.

"Sure, of course," I say. "Guess I don't have a monopoly on being unable to sleep."

"Give me a minute," Carson says, disappearing into the equipment room. He returns with a pair of well-worn CCMs.

I watch as he laces up with practiced efficiency. Not the precise movements of a pro, but the muscle memory is there.

"Played Division III in college," he offers, catching my look as he steps onto the ice. "I was never good enough for the show, but..." He takes a few experimental strides. "Some things you don't forget."

We skate in lazy circles for a while, the only sound is our skate blades cutting through fresh ice. It should feel strange—the GM joining my middle-of-the-night crisis skate—but somehow it doesn't. He doesn't seem compelled to make small talk, and I'm grateful. I guess the fact that we're both here in the middle of the damn night means we're past that?

"Used to do this in college," Carson says after a few laps. "Late nights when my head got too loud." He trails off, doing a passable backward crossover. "Makes it easier to think. Or maybe to stop thinking."

I catch the puck he slides my way, muscle memory taking over. We pass it back and forth, nothing fancy, just the hypnotic rhythm of tape to tape.

"You know," Carson says after a few quiet passes, "I used to think doing what was expected was the same as doing what was right. Be the good son, follow the expected path: college hockey, business degree, suitable marriage..." He trails off, his smile turning wistful. "Turns out there's a difference between living your life and going through the motions."

My stick stills on the ice as I look up at him. *Where is he going with this?*

"All I'm saying is," he sends another puck my way, "sometimes we spend so much time being who everyone needs us to be, we forget to figure out who we actually are."

Those words hit close to home. Isn't that what I've been doing for my whole damn life? Being the perfect captain, the responsible son, the steady teammate... But where has it gotten me?

"It's not that simple," I manage.

"No, it's not," he agrees quietly. "But you know what's harder? Spending the rest of your life wondering what might have been."

Something in his tone makes me look up sharply. For just a second, there's a shadow of old pain in his eyes, but he blinks and it's gone.

"Hockey careers end, Rylan," he continues softly. "Whether it's in two years or ten, someday you'll take those skates off for the last time. But living authentically? To be truly happy? That shit lasts forever."

The puck slides between us.

"I saw what happened to Jamie in Florida," I say finally. "The media circus, the pressure..."

"And you think that was worse than living a lie?" His voice is gentle but pointed. "Trust me, Rylan. No amount of professional success makes up for denying who you really are."

The edge in his voice makes me wonder what he's not saying, but he continues.

"You know what I first noticed about Pirelli when he was playing with the Jaguars?" He retrieves another puck, sending it over to me. "I mean, beyond his obvious talent? He never stopped trying. Even with all the shit he dealt with down there, with the team and the media. He kept showing up and doing his job. And he kept being himself through the whole shitstorm."

My throat tightens. Because that's Jamie. He's strong and brave. So much more than me.

"I'm sure it was hard," I manage. "Dealing with all of it..."

"Harder than hiding?" Carson's voice drops lower. "Harder than building walls so high you can't breathe behind them? Than living your life according to everyone else's expectations?"

The puck sits forgotten between us as his words sink in.

"Listen," he says after a moment, "I can't tell you what to do. But I can tell you that the path everyone expects you to take isn't always the right one. Sometimes..." he pauses, something flickering in his eyes. "Sometimes the hardest decisions are the ones that give us the most amazing outcomes."

"I don't know how to do this," I admit quietly. "How to be... this."

"Nobody does, at first." Carson skates closer. "But Rylan? Speaking from experience—it's better to face those hard truths now than to wake up twenty years later wondering who you might have been if you'd been brave enough to try."

We're quiet as those words hang in the air between us.

"I'll let you have the ice to yourself," Carson says finally, skating toward the boards. "But Rylan?"

I look up, catching something in his tone.

"The funny thing about living your life for other people? They're usually too busy living their own lives to notice your sacrifice." His smile holds a lifetime of understanding. "Don't wait twenty years to figure that out."

He's gone before I can respond, leaving me alone with the empty rink and the weight of his words.

The path everyone expects you to take isn't always the right one.

Nick's jersey hangs in my bedroom, preserved behind glass like all my careful walls. But Nick never lived behind glass. He lived fully, authentically, until the day he died.

And Jamie... Jamie's been living his truth since he was a teenager, paying the price but staying true to himself. While I've been hiding, controlling, and denying who I am for so long, I almost forgot who I am.

Almost.

My phone feels heavy in my hand as I pull it out. It's barely 5 AM—too early to call Dad in the rehab place. But in a few hours...

In a few hours, I'm going to stop living for everyone else's expectations.

In a few hours, I'm going to be brave.

Chapter 37

RYLAN

A couple of hours later, the rehab facility's number stares up at me from my phone screen. I've been sitting in my car in the practice facility parking lot for twenty minutes, watching the sunrise and trying to find the right words.

There aren't any. Not really.

My hands shake slightly as I dial. Two rings, then the now-familiar voice of the front desk coordinator. "Oceanview Recovery, how may I direct your call?"

"This is Rylan Collings. I'd like to speak with Roger Collings, please."

"One moment."

The hold music feels surreal, some soft jazz version of a pop song I vaguely recognize. Like this is just another call, not the moment I'm about to change everything.

"Rylan?" Dad's voice sounds clearer than it has in years. "Everything okay, son?"

"Yeah, I..." My throat closes up. "How are you?"

"Good, actually. I just finished my morning medi-
tation. Still feels weird, all this mindfulness stuff, b
ut..." He trails off. "You sure you're okay? You sound
strange."

"Dad, I need to tell you something." The words
come out in a rush. "And I need you to just... listen.
Okay?"

A pause. Then, softer: "Okay."

I take a deep breath, gripping the steering wheel
with my free hand. "I'm gay."

The silence stretches for one heartbeat, two...

"I know, son."

My breath catches. "What?"

"Your mother..." His voice catches slightly. "She
knew. Said we should wait until you were ready to tell
us. But then she... and Nick..." He clears his throat. "I
didn't handle any of it well."

"Dad..."

"Let me finish." There's a strength in his voice I
haven't heard in twenty years. "I failed you, Rylan.
After we lost them, I was so caught up in my own
grief, my own guilt... I couldn't be what you needed.
Couldn't create a safe space for you to be yourself."

Tears burn behind my eyes. "It's not your fault—"

"Some of it is." He sighs heavily. "But I'm trying to make amends now. Part of this recovery process is facing hard truths, and the truth is... I've known for a while that you were gay. Just didn't know how to talk about it. Shit, I haven't been able to talk about anything real for as long as I can remember."

"How long?" My voice is barely more than a whisper. "How long have you known?"

"You remember that summer after Nick died? When you stopped dating that girl?" A soft exhale. "The way you looked when people asked about her... it was the same look your mother used to get when she was trying to protect someone she loved."

My chest feels too tight. "Why didn't you ever say anything?"

"Christ, Rylan, I could barely say anything about anything back then." His laugh holds no humor. "And then your mother..." He stops and clears his throat. "Well. Let's just say alcohol became a very effective way to avoid conversations I didn't know how to have."

"Dad..."

"No, listen. Please." There's an urgency in his voice now. "I need to say this while I'm clear-headed enough to say it right. Your mother... she was so much better at this stuff. She knew how to create space for people to be themselves. After we lost her, I just... I failed you, son. Failed you both."

Both. Nick and me. The acknowledgment of that dual loss makes my eyes burn.

"Is there..." He pauses, and I can hear him choosing his words carefully. "Is there someone? Someone who makes you happy?"

Jamie's face flashes through my mind. His sunny smile, his patient understanding. The hurt in his eyes at yesterday's press conference...

"Yeah," I manage. "But I... I might have screwed it up."

"By trying to protect everyone else?" His voice is knowing. "By being the responsible one, like always?"

A sound escapes me that's half laugh, half sob. "Something like that."

"You know what I'm learning in here?" The rustling suggests he's settling into a chair. "We think we're protecting people when we hide parts of ourselves. But really, we're just... what did my counselor say? We're rejecting ourselves before others can.'"

"Sounds expensive," I joke weakly.

"Worth every penny if it helps me connect with my son." The raw honesty in his voice makes my throat tight. "Rylan... I know I haven't given you much reason to believe this, but... I love you. All of you. Even the parts you've been afraid to show me. I hope you can forgive me, and I hope you won't be afraid to be yourself with me anymore."

I sit in my car long after the call ends, watching the sun climb higher in the sky. Something fundamental has shifted. I can feel it. The walls I've built, the perfect control I've maintained... they don't feel like protection anymore. They feel like prison bars.

In a few hours, I have to face the team. Have to decide if I'm ready to be as brave as Jamie, and as authentic as Nick. As accepting of myself as my father is trying to be.

And for the first time in my life, the answer feels simple.

CHAPTER 38

RYLAN

Coach Shaw's voice fades in and out as he goes over our power play strategy. My pen moves across the page in precise lines, taking notes without processing the meaning of the words. Fifteen minutes left in the meeting. Fourteen. Thirteen.

Jamie's sitting in the back row. He hasn't looked at me once, but there are dark rings under his eyes. Because of me. I put those there yesterday when I hurt him with my cowardly words.

Louis shifts in his seat. He can always tell when something's off with me. But I keep my eyes forward, and my back straight. My armor's firmly in place. Just like always.

Ten more minutes.

Nine...

Eight...

My dad's voice from yesterday plays on a loop in my head: "We always knew, Ry. Your mother... she wanted to wait until you were ready to tell us."

Seven minutes.

Six...

Charlie's getting into some story about a restaurant mix-up, his British accent getting stronger as he gestures wildly. Normally I'd be smiling, but today I can hear him speak, but I'm not processing the words. There's too much other shit rattling around in my brain.

Lou's knee bumps mine under the desk. It's his usual subtle check-in when I'm too quiet. How many times has he been there for me over the years, while I kept on hiding? I don't know what I did to deserve him, but I could never ask for a better friend.

Three...

Two...

My heart is racing like a fucking *Formula One* car as Coach Shaw wraps up and asks if anyone has anything to add. This is it.

One...

Time to stop hiding.

"Yeah." My voice sounds a lot steadier than I feel. I get out of my chair and turn so I'm facing everyone. Lou sucks in a breath. "There's something I need to say."

The room goes quiet. Even Charlie stops fidgeting. In the back row, Jamie finally looks at me, and the raw hope in his eyes nearly steals my voice.

I clear my throat. "I've been your captain for three and a half years." My tone is neutral. It's like I'm talking about line changes or killing power plays, not making a life-altering announcement. "And in that time, I've asked you for your trust, your respect, and your honesty."

I suck in a deep breath.

"But I haven't done the same for you. And it's time that changes."

The silence in the room thickens. Someone, Santucci, maybe, shifts in their chair.

"I'm gay."

JAMIE

Rylan's words hang in the air like smoke after a fireworks show.

After yesterday's press conference, I convinced myself that I've been imagining everything between us. Thinking I somehow read too much into every touch, every night together, every moment with Rylan over the last couple of months. But now...

The room is so quiet I can hear the hum of the fluorescent lights. Rylan stands perfectly still at the front of the room. His face is pale, probably from nerves, but he keeps his head up and his grey-blue eyes look like steel. He's ready and braced for whatever hits he might have to take.

Charlie's first to break the silence. "What..." He clears his throat and tries again. "Fucking hell, mate. Why didn't you tell us before?"

"I know this might change how some of you feel about my leadership," Rylan continues. "I'll understand if anyone has a prob—"

"Oh no, fuck that noise," Louis interrupts, standing up. "You're our captain. End of story."

A murmur of agreement ripples through the room.

Austin stands, and for one horrible second, I think he's going to walk out. But he moves toward Rylan instead. He's wearing his usual scowl, but I think that ornery look is hiding a load of emotions right now. "You're the best team captain I've ever played with," he says finally. "Nothing changes that. Anyone who has a problem with this is going to have to deal with me."

They exchange a hug, and the look on Rylan's face is pure relief mixed with gratitude.

"Should've told us sooner, Cap," Santucci rumbles from his seat in the corner. "Could've set you up with my cousin, Marco. He's a doctor."

A surprised laugh escapes Rylan, and the smile on his face is one of his rare genuine ones. He's so fucking gorgeous when he's happy.

"I appreciate the thought, Santucci, but..." His eyes find mine again. "I'm actually... taken..."

My heart stops.

"Jamie and I…" He takes a deep breath. "We're… together. I mean, I hope we are. But either way, I'm done hiding."

Just then, Carson Wells clears his throat from where he's standing at the back of the room. I must have missed him coming in.

"The team stands behind both of you. Completely." His eyes sweep the room. "If anyone has a problem, you come see me."

"Fuck that," Louis says cheerfully. "They'll have to get through us first." He stands to wrap his best friend in a bear hug, and just like that, the tension in the room shatters.

I'm moving before I realize it. As I make my way down to the front of the room, Austin catches my eye for a moment before dipping his chin in my direction. I take it as both a blessing and a warning all at once.

Louis releases Rylan, who watches me approach with wide, vulnerable eyes.

"Hey." My voice is rough. Everything I want to say crowds my throat: how proud I am, how brave he is, how fucking much I love him. But the only thing that comes out is, "You okay?"

A small, tentative smile crosses his face. "I don't know yet." He reaches for my hand and squeezes it hard. "But I think I will be."

The room erupts around us. Charlie starts calling for a celebration party at Bigfoot's, as Coach Shaw gathers his notes with a satisfied smile. Louis has a proud smile on his face as he chats with Tanner, and the group of rookies in the back start talking about some video game tournament they're running among themselves.

But I barely notice any of it. Because Rylan's hand is still in mine, and for the first time since I've known him, his captain's mask is nowhere to be found.

"Jamie..." he starts, but Charlie interrupts by throwing an arm around both our shoulders.

"Right then! We're going for drinks at Bigfoot's. No arguments! This calls for a proper celebration."

"He's right." Louis's voice is rough, but there's a proud smile on his face. "Plus, you owe us drinks for keeping this secret for so long."

"Deal," Rylan laughs, his fingers tightening around mine. "But I think we might need a minute first."

Louis immediately starts herding everyone toward the door, ignoring Charlie's protests. "Come on, you animals. Let's go, first round's on me. We'll save you both a seat," he calls over his shoulder, pulling the door closed behind him.

As the room empties, Rylan turns to face me. His hand trembles in mine, but his eyes are clear and sure. Like he's found his way home.

And somehow I just know we're going to be okay.

CHAPTER 39

RYLAN

The makeup artist's brush feels strange against my skin as the studio bustles with pre-broadcast activity. Just twenty-four hours ago, I was sitting in my car, gathering the courage to call my dad. Now I'm about to come out to the entire world.

"Nervous?" Declan asks quietly, adjusting his suit jacket. The usual rumpled journalist is polished today, ready for the live broadcast.

"Weirdly, I'm not." After telling my dad and then my team, this part feels almost like an afterthought. Almost.

My phone buzzes with a text from Jamie.

> *Ready whenever you are, baby.*

He's waiting in another room to join us later. The endearment makes my chest warm, even as reality hits me again. A few months ago, I could barely look at

Jamie Pirelli without panic. Now we're about to tell the world we're together.

"And we're live in 5... 4... 3..."

"I'm here with Seattle Sasquatch captain Rylan Collings," Declan starts smoothly. "Rylan, thank you for choosing to share your story with us today."

"Thanks for having me." My media voice kicks in automatically, but I force myself to soften it. No more perfect captain's mask. That's the whole point.

"You've led the Sasquatch to significant success, including a Stanley Cup. But today, you want to talk about something more personal."

Deep breath. This is it. "That's right. I've spent my entire life hiding an important part of who I am. There have been some changes recently that have made me realize it's time to stop hiding." My hands grip my knees under the desk, my knuckles white. But when I say the two words, my voice is clear and strong despite my racing pulse. "I'm gay."

The words feel different here than they did with my dad and the team. More final. More real. My chest tightens, but not with panic—with something that feels surprisingly like relief.

"That's not an easy thing to share in pro sports," Declan says matter-of-factly. "Why now?"

I think about Jamie's smile this morning. About my dad's acceptance and about Nick's old jersey hanging on my wall.

"It's time. The league's done a lot to show they're welcoming, but we all know locker rooms aren't always the most accepting places." I lean forward slightly. "I'm tired of hiding."

"Before we continue, I'd like to acknowledge something," Declan says carefully. "You've given me permission to talk about your brother Nick, who many hockey fans might remember as one of the most promising prospects of his generation before his tragic death in a car accident almost twenty years ago."

My chest tightens at hearing Nick discussed so publicly, but I nod. This is part of why I'm here. "Yeah. Nick was... he was incredible. Not just as a player. Everyone talked about him being the next Gretzky, but he was so much more than that. He was my big brother."

"Your brother Nick knew about your sexuality, didn't he?" Declan asks gently.

My throat tightens, but in a good way. "Yeah. He was... he was incredible about it. I was pretty young, and I was just figuring things out right before his accident." I swallow hard as memories of that last summer with Nick wash over me. "But I talked to him about it one night, before he left for college. Looking back, I think he might have known even before I did. Nick always saw right through my walls."

"That must have had a profound impact on you."

"Nick was always completely himself. Never afraid to be exactly who he was. After we lost him, and then my mom a year later... it was easier to focus on anything other than the pain. Hockey helped me push it all away." I meet Declan's eyes. "But that's not really living, is it?"

"No," he agrees. "It's not."

"My father's in recovery now," I continue, the words flowing easier. "He's facing some hard truths about himself. And watching him do that work... I realized I need to do the same."

"Jamie Pirelli joined the team this season. Did that influence your decision?"

My heart races at Jamie's name, and I can't stop a small laugh. "Yeah, it did. Actually..." I take a deep breath, ready to share something I've never said aloud before. "Jamie reminds me of Nick sometimes. Not just on the ice, though they share that incredible hockey sense. It's... it's the way he lives so authentically. The way he makes everyone around him feel safe to be themselves."

I swallow hard. "Nick would have loved him. And I think... I think Nick would be proud of me. I'm finally following his example. Being brave enough to be myself."

"Jamie Pirelli made history as the first openly bisexual player drafted into the NHL. And I understand he's waiting to join us?"

I don't even try to hold back my smile. "Yeah, he is."

"Before we bring him out, tell me, what was your initial reaction when he was traded to Seattle?"

Another laugh escapes. "Honestly? I was terrified. Not because of his reputation. I was scared because from the moment he walked in, I knew he was going to change everything."

"Jamie," Declan calls out. "Why don't you join us?"

My heart thuds as Jamie walks out. He looks unfairly good in dark jeans and a sweater that makes his eyes impossibly blue. Heat crawls up my neck as his media-ready smile softens into a genuine one when our eyes meet. My whole body leans toward him instinctively before I catch myself.

"Hi," he says simply, settling beside me. His hand finds my knee off-camera, grounding me.

"Jamie, you've been through your own journey with being out in pro sports," Declan says. "What's it like being on this side of things?"

Jamie's thumb traces circles on my knee as he answers. "It's incredible. When I first came out, I hoped it might make things easier for other players, but I never expected..." He glances at me, expression soft. "I never expected to find this."

"So you two are...?"

"We're together," I say firmly. "It's new, but it's..." I look at Jamie, thinking about that first night in San Diego, that video call, the careful distance between us, and the ultimate choice to be brave. "It's everything."

"The chemistry between you on ice has been remarkable," Declan says. "Has your personal connection enhanced that?"

Jamie grins. "Rylan makes me better. On and off the ice."

"Even when I'm driving you crazy with my color-coded sock drawer?" The chirp slips out without thinking.

"Your sock drawer is a masterpiece," he teases.

"Any message for young players out there?" Declan asks.

Jamie's hand finds mine, not caring that it's in frame. "Be yourself. When you find the right team, the right people... they'll rally around you the way a team's supposed to. No one will care who you love as long as that person makes you happy."

"It's worth it," I add softly. "Being authentic, being brave... it's terrifying, but it's worth it."

"Any final thoughts?"

I look at Jamie, seeing how far we've come right there in his eyes. "I'm grateful. To the organization, our teammates, the fans who've been so supportive... but mostly..." I squeeze his hand and clear my throat. "Mostly, I'm grateful I don't have to choose between the game I love and the person I love."

Jamie's breath catches as I realize what I just said. To the entire world... My heart pounds so hard the microphones must pick it up. Heat floods my face as the words echo in my head. *The person I love.*

"And we're clear!"

The energy shifts as crew members move around, but I'm frozen, the words echoing in my head—*the person I love.*

"Well," Declan stands with a knowing smile. "I think that went well. Thanks guys. The studio's booked for another hour. Take your time." Then he's gone, herding the crew out with surprising efficiency.

The moment we're alone, Jamie turns to me. "Did you mean it?"

"I..." My media-polished vocabulary fails me when faced with his hopeful blue eyes. "I didn't plan to tell you like that—on camera. But... Yeah. Yeah, I meant it."

His smile could light up the whole damn city. "Good. Because I love you too."

"Even with my color-coded sock drawer?" I try teasing, but my voice is rough.

"Especially with your color-coded sock drawer." He leans in, pressing his forehead to mine. "I love every ridiculously organized, perfectly controlled, surprisingly soft part of you, Rylan Collings."

"Jamie..."

"Not only did you just come out, you also casually dropped the L-word in front of the entire world," he whispers. "How are you still standing?"

A laugh escapes me. "I'm pretty sure I'm a mess. But maybe..." I squeeze his hand. "Maybe that's okay sometimes."

His blue eyes sparkle. "It's very much okay."

CHAPTER 40

JAMIE

After our interview, everything feels different. Even our basic pre-game skate carries a new energy that makes my skin tingle. The tension we were dreading isn't there, instead, there's something protective, almost celebratory radiating from the team. Louis casually positions himself between us and the media section while we stretch, batting his eyelashes innocently while deliberately mishearing every shouted question. Charlie chatters non-stop about some new coffee shop he discovered, his British accent getting progressively thicker as he creates a wall of words between us and the press. Even Austin, Mr. Gruff-and-Tough, has transformed himself into an aggressively protective barrier; his usual scowl turned outward like a shield.

I can't stop stealing glances at Rylan. After three months of careful distance, being able to watch him openly is intoxicating. The way his face settles into that intense focus during drills. The familiar rhythm of his skating that I've memorized but had to pretend not to notice. Now I can look and appreciate without having to hide. My heart races every time he glances at me with that private smile playing at the corners of his mouth.

"Pirelli." Coach's voice cuts through my Rylan-induced haze. "We're running that new power play setup in tonight's game. You ready?"

"Yes, Coach." My voice is steady, despite the flutter in my chest when Rylan's gaze meets mine. His eyes hold his usual intensity, but there's something lighter there now, like a weight has lifted.

A reporter shouts a question about our relationship. Austin immediately appears between us and the boards, all six-foot-three of him radiating 'try me' energy.

"Media availability is after the game tonight," Louis calls out cheerfully, but there's steel under his smile. "Though I think I heard you asking about Charlie's new coffee obsession? He'd love to tell you all about proper brewing temperatures!"

Charlie perks up. "Well, actually, the optimal temperature for extraction is..."

A few hours later, the locker room buzzes with pre-game energy. Rylan maintains his captain's composure, but there's something softer about him now. His movements are just as precise, but somehow they feel more natural, less rigid. When our eyes meet across the room, he doesn't look away. Instead, that private little smile appears, the one that used to be reserved for hotel rooms and hidden moments.

"Last game before Christmas break," Charlie announces, practically bouncing as he re-tapes his stick for the fifteenth time. "Let's give the fans something to remember, yeah?"

Something to remember. Three days ago, we were terrified of anyone knowing about us. Now Rylan's hand brushes mine as he passes, a deliberate touch that sends electricity through my entire body. No more hiding. No more pretending not to notice how perfectly we fit together, on and off the ice.

"Neutral zone!" Rylan's voice cuts through the crowd noise as I track the puck. His captain's tone hasn't changed, but knowing I can look at him now, really look at him, sharpens everything. The pass connects perfectly, like always. Like our passes almost always do, since that first practice when our chemistry was undeniable. Now everyone knows why.

We're up 2-0 heading into the third period. The crowd's energy seems different tonight, or maybe I'm just allowing myself to notice it more. During warmups, I spotted two teenage boys holding hands while wearing matching Sasquatch hoodies. My throat tightened at the sight of them. This is exactly what I dreamed about when I first came out at nineteen. The reason I fought through those brutal years in Florida, to get to what I found here, with Rylan, with this team. Against all odds.

"Nice feed," Austin grunts as we change lines. Coming from him, it's practically a love sonnet.

A young girl pressed against the glass catches my eye. She's wearing my jersey and Rylan's, somehow taped together into one piece. When I wave, her whole face lights up, and my vision goes a little blurry. All those years of being one of the few out players, and now here's a kid wearing both our jerseys together, like it's the most natural thing in the world.

"Hey, Pirelli, save the heartwarming stuff for after we win this thing," Louis chirps as we head back out, smacking my ass with his goalie stick.

The win, when it comes, feels bigger than this one game. Rylan finds me in the celebration, and for the first time, neither of us pulls away too quickly. The team piles on, creating a bubble of protection around us. I catch glimpses of rainbow signs in the crowd, of kids jumping up and down wearing both our jerseys.

This is what change feels like.

RYLAN

A while later, after we've cooled down and showered, Jamie and I head out of the locker room. My hand keeps brushing his as we walk, each touch sending sparks through my body. No more pretending these touches are accidental. No more carefully maintaining distance.

"Um, Rylan? Jamie?"

The tentative voice stops us. A teenager, maybe fifteen or sixteen, stands clutching a Sasquatch jersey with trembling hands. One of the few fans with post-game access passes. But when they hold up the jersey, my breath catches. Someone has carefully combined our names, "PIRELLI-COLLINGS" stretched across the shoulders. The sight hits me like a body check, knocking the air from my lungs.

"Nice jersey," Jamie says softly beside me, his voice warm. The kid's entire face lights up, and something in my chest tightens.

"I... I made it myself. After your interview." Their voice shakes slightly. "I just—thank you. For coming out. It means a lot, showing everyone that you can be queer and still play great hockey."

"Yeah." My voice comes out gentler than usual, as memories of my own teenage years flooding back. Hiding in our small northern Ontario town, watching hockey with Nick while desperately trying to suppress who I was. "You definitely can."

The kid's parent hovers nearby, giving us a watery smile as they snap a photo. After they leave, my hand finds Jamie's, seeking his solid warmth. Three months ago, I wouldn't have even dreamed about this. Now his touch grounds me, like an anchor in this whirlwind of emotion.

"You okay?" Jamie asks quietly, and I realize my eyes are burning.

"Yeah, just..." I squeeze his hand, trying to organize the overwhelming flood of feelings into words. "When I was that age, hiding in our small town... I never thought I'd see anything like this. Never could have dreamed I could have this."

Jamie's eyes go soft, and I think about how far we've both come. Me from that terrified kid in Ontario, him from that brave nineteen-year-old coming out before getting drafted. Both of us finding each other here, now.

"We're doing it," he murmurs, his voice thick with emotion. "Helping people. Maybe we're not arguing cases before the Supreme Court like Lola, or building rockets like Edward, or being brain surgeons like Adam, but we're doing important stuff. We're showing kids they don't have to choose between hockey and being themselves."

I give him a soft smile. No more captain's mask, no more careful control. Just me, just us. "Yeah," I say, squeezing his hand again. "Yeah, we are."

The team's waiting at Bigfoot's Sin Bin, which is quickly becoming our unofficial victory spot. Charlie's animated voice carries across the room as he demonstrates his "brilliant" media deflection techniques. Louis catches my eye as we walk in, and the smile he gives me almost feels like pride. Even Austin's usual scowl has softened into something that almost looks like contentment.

I keep hold of Jamie's hand as we join them. No more carefully orchestrated distance or rigid control. Just us, surrounded by our chosen family, celebrating not just tonight's win but everything that led us here. Three months ago, I was suffocating behind walls built out of fear and loss. Now I feel as though I can breathe freely—maybe for the first time since Nick died.

"Hey." My voice is low, meant just for Jamie. When he looks at me, the love in his eyes makes my heart race. "Come home with me tonight?"

The word 'home' feels different now. It's not just my meticulously organized apartment, it's somewhere we both belong. Jamie leans closer, giving me a filthy smile that's full of promise. It's enough to make me forget about everyone around us. "Always," he whispers.

What we've found is more than acceptance or visibility or even love. We've found home. In each other, in this team, in this city that's embraced us both. And maybe that's the biggest win of all.

Epilogue
Two Months Later:
RYLAN

The rehab clinic looks like a cozy cluster of cottages in the in the winter sunlight, with snow dusting the evergreens surrounding the like powdered sugar. The crisp mountain air reminds me of early morning practices back home, but without the crushing weight of expectations that used to sit on my chest. Everything looks different now—cleaner and brighter. Or maybe it's just Dad who looks different. He's clear-eyed and present in a way I haven't seen since before we lost Nick, his shoulders relaxed instead of hunched over with guilt.

"The team's playing well," Dad says, pushing a coffee across the table with steady hands—hands that don't shake anymore. "Been watching all the games. That power-play goal against Edmonton last night was something else."

The casual way he talks about hockey now, actually following the games instead of drowning them out with whiskey, makes my chest warm. "Yeah, we're really clicking. Carson thinks he can keep the core group together if we keep performing like this."

"Good. Though..." Dad's expression turns knowing, reminding me so much of how he used to look when he coached minor hockey. "Lou seemed a bit off in the third. Tremblay usually makes those glove saves look easy."

I blink, surprised by his observation. A year ago, he wouldn't have noticed anything beyond his own grief. But he's right; Lou's been favoring his right side lately, though he keeps insisting he's fine. "Maybe. He's, uh, probably just tired."

Dad nods, not pushing. That's another change: he's learning when to let things breathe. "So," his smile turns slightly nervous, like Nick's used to before big games. "Jamie's coming up with you next time, right?"

My heart does that weird flippy thing it always does when someone mentions Jamie. "If you're sure you're ready. We can wait—"

"No, I want to meet him properly." Dad's voice is firm and steady. He pulls a book from beside his chair, handling it like something precious. "Alexandra's been..." He pauses, choosing his words carefully, which is another new habit. "She's been so kind. Sent me some resources and said I could call her anytime. Even suggested some support groups in Vancouver for when I finish the program."

I catch the title: *"Supporting Your LGBTQ+ Child: A Guide for Parents."* The Post-it notes sticking out of various pages are covered in Alexandra's distinctive handwriting. Through the clear plastic of the sleeve, I can see one note that reads: "Remember: progress isn't linear, but love is constant."

"She's not..." I search for the right words, protective of this fragile new peace between us. "She's not overwhelming you?"

Dad's laugh is genuine—a sound I'd almost forgotten existed. "No, she's... she's good at reading people. Knows when to push and when to step back." He looks down at the book, running his fingers along the spine. "Actually, I've been thinking... There's a good outpatient program here in Vancouver. And the winters are easier than back home..."

My heart skips. "Dad?"

"Might be nice," he says carefully, like he's testing ice thickness. "Being closer. Getting a fresh start. And your Jamie's family seems to visit Seattle pretty often ..."

"They'd love having you closer," I say softly, thinking of how Alexandra lights up whenever she talks about "chosen family." "We all would."

His eyes get misty, but they're clear, not glazed with alcohol or grief. "Your mother would have loved all this, you know. The Pirellis, Jamie... she always said you needed someone who could make you laugh. Make you less..." He gestures vaguely at me, a hint of teasing in his voice. "Rigid."

"Yeah?" Something in my chest loosens at hearing him talk about Mom without immediately reaching for a drink.

"Oh, yeah." He smiles, and it reaches his eyes. He taps the book. "Alexandra said something about Jamie wanting to reorganize your kitchen?"

I groan, but I'm smiling too. "He says my organizational system 'suffocates the space.' Can you believe that? My perfectly labeled—"

"Storage containers might benefit from a little chaos?" Dad's eyes twinkle. "Smart boy, that Jamie."

"Dad..." I roll my eyes, loving this teasing side of him I haven't seen since I was a kid.

"I know, I know." He reaches across the table, his hand steady and warm as it covers mine. "I just... I'm glad you found someone who sees you. Really sees you." His voice roughens. "I'm sorry it took me so long to do the same."

My eyes burn with tears I'm no longer afraid to show. "You're here now, Dad. That's what matters."

A little while later, when I hug him goodbye, I breathe in the scent of soap and coffee instead of stale whiskey. I love it.

As I get into my car for the drive back down I-5 to Seattle, my phone buzzes with Jamie's distinctive tone. He's sent a photo of what appears to be multiple Italian cookbooks spread across his coffee table, sticky notes and penciled annotations visible on the pages. The caption reads:

> Deciding on some treats to make for your Dad. We'll ease him into the Pirelli chaos one step at a time. Drive safe, baby. Love you.

My heart squeezes with joy, something that's been happening more and more often lately. Everything's falling into place in a way I could have never imagined. Never even could have hoped for. Dad's making incredible progress in his recovery, things with the team are clicking, and my relationship with Jamie is... amazing.

I've been playing some of the best hockey of my entire career. Jamie and I are creating plays that should be impossible, but somehow they work because we read each other so well. Since Christmas break, the team's record is well above .500, and as the All-Star break draws closer, the Evertons are apparently pleased.

I'm learning the best things in life can't be controlled, or organized, or put into neat little boxes. Jamie's brand of chaos and sunshine makes me feel alive, and for the first time since Nick and my mom died, I feel... steady. Anchored. Those walls I spent years building, thinking they were protecting me? They were just keeping all the good stuff out.

It's still early, but Jamie and I are building something good together. I know, deep down in my gut, that no matter what life throws at us next, we'll get through it. Together.

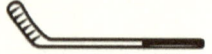

Thanks so much for reading Rylan! I hope you loved Rylan & Jamie's story!

Curious about goalies Lou and Tanner? Their story is out now!

Louis: Seattle Sasquatch Hockey Book 2
Two Goalies, one net, and a game they never saw coming.

Get it at https://getbook.at/LOUIS (case sensitive)

Also check out the *Hot Dam Homes* series.

From The Ground Up is a steamy, hurt-comfort, celebrity-blue collar romance.

https://mybook.to/ftgu(case sensitive)

Books & Stories by Harper Robson

The Hot Dam Homes Series

From The Ground Up
https://mybook.to/ftgu
When The Walls Come Down
https://mybook.to/whenthewallscomedown
Built To Last
https://getbook.at/builttolast
An Unexpected Gift: A Hot Dam Homes Christmas Novella
https://getbook.at/AUG

The Seattle Sasquatch Series

Rylan: Book One
https://getbook.at/rylan(case sensitive)
Louis: Book Two
https://getbook.at/LOUIS (case sensitive)
The Night Before, A Seattle Sasquatch Holiday
Prequel:
https://mybook.to.tnb(case sensitive)
Carson: Book Three (2026)
https://mybook.to/CARSON (case sensitive)
Book Four (2026)

The Getaways Series

Making Waves

https://mybook.to/makingwaves
Love After Love, A Getaways Novella
https://mybook.to/loveafterlove

All books are available on Amazon and in Kindle Unlimited

All About Harper Robson

Harper Robson grew up dreaming about being a writer someday. That someday didn't arrive until she was in her mid-forties—better late than never, right? While on the journey she worked in marketing, software development, the oil & gas industry and spent more than a decade as a stay-home mom. She grew up in Vancouver, BC, but feels most at home in the leafy green suburbs of Seattle, Washington. In 2023, Harper and her clan pulled up stakes and headed south to live in Southern California. She was certain she'd miss the cozy, rainy, Pacific Northwest, but it turns out regular doses of sunshine and palm trees are pretty easy to get used to and San Diego feels more like home every day.

She's a mom to two teenaged boys and an adorable but naughty yellow Labrador Retriever. Her husband works in the tech industry and he makes her laugh every single day.

A true PNW girl, Harper loves the rain but is always planning her next beach vacation. Her favorite things include road trips, classic rock, the Seattle Kraken, her dogs, and drinking champagne for no reason at all.

She would love to hear from you! Email her at harper@harperrobson.com

Visit harperrobson.com and sign up for the Newsletter

Let's Connect!

The best way to keep up with all things Harper is to sign up for the VIP Newsletter:
https://www.subscribepage.com/harpernewsletter

Bluesky: @harperrobsonauthor.bsky.social
Facebook: Harper Robson
Instagram: @harperrobsonauthor
BookBub: @harperrobsonauthor
Goodreads:
https://www.goodreads.com/author/show/2228446
9.Harper_Robson

Amazon Author Page

https://www.amazon.com/author/harperrobson

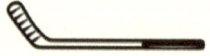

Website: www.harperrobson.com